WAR CLOUDS OVER WEST FLORIDA

WAR CLOUDS OVER WEST FLORIDA

Lee Gramling

PINEAPPLE PRESS, INC.
Palm Beach, Florida

For Frank and the rest of the Gainesville breakfast bunch.

Pineapple Press
Published by Rowman & Littlefield
An imprint of The Rowman & Littlefield Publishing Group, Inc.
4501 Forbes Blvd., Ste. 200
Lanham, MD 20706
www.rowman.com

Distributed by NATIONAL BOOK NETWORK

ISBN 978-1-68334-063-8 (paperback)
ISBN 978-1-68334-064-5 (e-book)

British Library Cataloguing in Publication Information Available

Library of Congress Cataloging-in-Publication Data Available

Library of Congress Control Number: 2019953084

∞™ The paper used in this publication meets the minimum requirements of American National Standard for Information Sciences—Permanence of Paper for Printed Library Materials, ANSI/NISO Z39.48-1992.

THANKS

To Cate at the Margaret Key Library in Apalachicola and Megan at the Apala-chicola Maritime Museum; both ladies were bright spots during my research trip to west Florida several years ago. Many thanks also to June and David Cussen for not forgetting me during my long hiatus from writing. And to the friends mentioned in my dedication—Frank, Parker, Al, Harley, and others—for their ongoing encouragement. A special thanks to Bill Little for his kind words, which finally got me behind the keyboard again. And last but not least, a grateful fist-bump to my editor Debra Murphy for her remarkable patience.

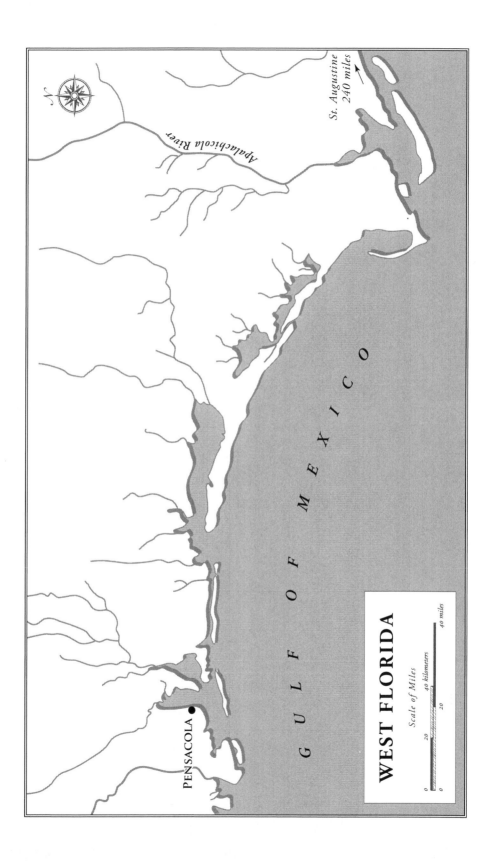

St. Augustine
240 miles

Apalachicola River

G U L F   O F   M E X I C O

PENSACOLA

WEST FLORIDA

Scale of Miles

0   20   40 miles

0   20   40 kilometers

1

It couldn't properly be called a cabin, Kirkland decided. It was much too large, for one thing. And it appeared far better constructed than those other rough structures he'd seen on the frontier, both in the States and among the Cracker settlements in these Spanish colonies of Florida.

It was made of logs, to be sure, but these had been squared off and fitted together so well that there was hardly a need for any filler between them. And it was a full two stories high, set well off the ground with broad verandas at the front and rear extending across the entire width of the house. These were roofed over with cypress shingles and well shaded at the sides by cedars and wax myrtles. A low parapet around the roof edge contained loopholes, which gave it the appearance of a kind of frontier fort.

Just in front of the two men and a little to the right of the grove of fruit trees where they'd reined in their horses was a grape arbor with a wrought-iron bench beneath it. The vines were barren twigs now in the latter part of February. But there would be a time when their leafy shade offered a welcome retreat from the heat of summer.

They could also make out cultivated plots on either side of the broad steps leading up to the veranda. Only a few scattered blue and yellow specks of color among the bare folds of earth gave any suggestion of the riot of flowers that would likely fill such places once spring arrived.

Ever since early yesterday they had ridden past great expanses of grassland where long-horned cattle clustered about, grazing or lying at rest. They'd also passed fallow fields where corn and other crops would soon await the new season.

It was an impressive freehold, everything considered—here in the middle of what everyone in the North seemed to believe was no more than a barren untamed wilderness. Its existence said a lot about the man whose planning and determination lay behind it. And knowing this, Kirkland admitted to himself, was more than a little bit daunting.

That man was the one he'd traveled more than a thousand miles to see.

Thin columns of smoke were now rising into the late-afternoon sky from two dun brick chimneys at each end of the house. It was a sign that the residents were at home anyway, a hopeful thing after all those long days they'd spent aboard ship and on horseback.

"Well, Sergeant," Kirkland told his companion quietly, "I suppose we may as well go ahead and brook the old lion in his den."

"No time like the present, sir," the other agreed.

They walked their mounts forward to a matched pair of hitching posts that stood alongside the front steps. Next to each was a hollowed-out log that served as a watering trough. Once they'd dismounted, they tied the reins with enough slack so the animals could reach the troughs to drink.

Kirkland removed his beaver hat and did the best he could to knock the dust of travel from it and his clothes. The man beside him did the same.

Then, after sharing a glance and a curt nod of something resembling decision, they mounted the steps to the veranda.

Kirkland stepped across it and rapped on the door.

A few minutes earlier, on the other side of that door, John Thomas Mac-Kenzie had taken his place at the massive table at one end of the large open living area for dinner with his family. The table was a single great slab of virgin cypress, handcrafted and lovingly polished by his own hands these many years since. He took pride in his workmanship, as he did in every part of this Florida *rancho* he'd created.

But none of it compared in the least to the pride he felt in the family now sitting on either side of him. He unfolded his napkin and sat back in his chair with a contented smile as he let his eyes travel from one to the other of the younger people at the table.

To his right and left were his two tall sons, John Robert and Jeremiah. Each showed clear signs of proving himself at least as strong and capable as his father. John Robert, the oldest, had already begun taking an interest in the day-to-day management of the *rancho*. Jeremiah was younger and perhaps not yet so responsible. But his skills with weapons, horses, and the tracking of game were even now as great as (or greater than) MacKenzie's had been at that age.

Next to John Robert was his wife, Mary, a recent and welcome addition to the MacKenzie clan. Dark haired and lovely, she'd received more education than all the rest of them combined. It was pleasing to see how she'd already started adding a touch of much-needed refinement to this rough-and-ready frontier household.

She saw her father-in-law looking at her and smiled back, meeting his eyes boldly. For all of what some might consider her fashionable breeding, she was no shy or delicate flower. She'd taken to frontier life with competence and zest— and with few, if any, noticeable regrets.

Across from Mary was MacKenzie's only daughter, Rebecca, the youngest of the brood. Everyone but him, it seemed, just called her Becky. When his eyes came to her she favored him with a grin, and he beamed at her in return. She was without question the apple of his eye, and he made no bones about it. It had always struck him with wonder that any lass so pretty could have sprung from his own loins.

Of course, she did have her late mother's eyes. But her copper-colored hair she owed to him—along with the freckles on her cheeks and nose, which she seemed to resent. These, he knew, would fade with time. He wished he could be so sure about the bold and reckless spirit that she'd also inherited from him. It was a trait that gave him pause from time to time.

Steaming dishes of food were brought in by Maria and Carlos, MacKenzie's two longtime household employees. Then everyone held hands while Mary said the customary grace.

MacKenzie picked up the carving knife to start on the roast, and the others began passing their plates forward to where he sat at the head of the table.

The three sharp raps on the outside door sounded uncommonly loud in the winter stillness. No evening visitors had been expected.

While friendly guests were always welcome in the MacKenzie home, this was still for the most part an untamed frontier. Beyond the immediate precincts of the few Spanish towns and military posts, there were roving bands of outlaws, runaway slaves, and even at times some hostile Indians. Guarded caution was a well-founded habit.

MacKenzie glanced at his sons, who had already started to rise from their seats. They went to the wall next to the great stone fireplace and took their flint-lock rifles from their brackets.

Their sister made a move to stand up as well, but a terse "Rebecca!" from her father made her pause to look his way. He gestured her back to her seat, and after a moment she grudgingly complied.

Carlos and Maria had reappeared at the entrance from the kitchen, curious but also ready in case the late arrivals should prove hostile. Carlos held a large cleaver in his hand, and Maria was hefting a heavy iron skillet.

MacKenzie pushed his chair back and went to the door, taking a position a little to one side of it.

"Who is it without there that knocks?" he called. "An' what is it y' might be wantin' at this hour o' the evenin'?"

"Two visitors from the United States," came the immediate reply, "who have come a very long distance to speak with Mister MacKenzie." There was a pause, then, "We're both of us friendly."

"It is MacKenzie y're now speakin' to. What business is it y' might have wi' me?"

"We'll be very happy to explain if we're allowed to come inside. It's a little bit cold out here for long conversations."

MacKenzie looked at his sons, who stood back from the entrance with their weapons pointed toward it. "Well enough," he said with a nod of decision. "We've always a welcome for visitors, just so long as they may prove friendly."

He lifted the heavy bolt and pushed it to one side, then swung the door inward and took a step away from it.

2

The young man who stood framed in the doorway was tall and clean shaven, wearing a long blue overcoat that was now unbuttoned to reveal a slim tailored black suit and Boston boots that came almost to the knee. He held a beaver hat in his hand.

Behind him was a somewhat older man, dressed in clothes more like those of a frontiersman: coarse woolen trousers and a hunting shirt under a still-buttoned, knee-length buckskin jacket. His sideburns were long and flecked with gray but appeared to have been recently trimmed. His chin was bare of stubble.

Neither man had any weapons in sight. Jeremiah and John Robert lowered their rifles.

MacKenzie gestured them inside and rebarred the door. "Have y' eaten?" he asked, turning back.

"Not since early this morning," the younger man said with a smile.

"Then seat y'selves at table. We'll save business affairs for after."

They all approached the table. But before pulling out the offered chair, the younger man halted a step away and bowed courteously to Mary and Becky.

"I believe introductions would be in order first. I am Lieutenant Charles Andrew Kirkland of the United States Navy. And this"—he indicated his companion—"is Gunnery Sergeant Nehemiah Jaynes of the US Marines."

Mary smiled and offered her hand while MacKenzie raised an eyebrow at the mention of military ranks. Becky, across the table, belatedly offered her own hand as well.

After lightly grasping each hand between his fingers, Kirkland removed his long coat and handed it to the waiting Carlos, who already held the sergeant's buckskin jacket. Still standing, he turned to his host. "As you might guess, we have both come here to Florida incognito. But we mean no harm by that, neither to the Spanish government nor to any of its subjects. Quite the contrary, in fact."

MacKenzie resumed his seat and indicated for his guests to take theirs. "I'll be very interested to hear how it is y' explain that," he said, "when once we have supped. But our food begins to grow cold, an' in my house hospitality comes first. All other matters after."

His sons replaced their rifles and came to join them. The remaining introductions were quickly completed while Maria set two additional places at the table.

Then everyone devoted their full attention to a generous and well-prepared meal that confirmed everything Kirkland had earlier guessed about the prolific success of his host's *rancho* out here in the Florida wilderness.

There was very little talk until coffee had been brought, along with a "wee dram" of Scottish whiskey for each of the men at the table. MacKenzie sat back in his chair and filled his pipe, eying his guests thoughtfully while he puffed it to life.

"Well now," he said as the blue smoke made its way into the rafters, "y' may tell us finally—wi' no mincin' o' words—what it is that might bring two military men from yon land to the north down here into Spanish Florida."

Kirkland noticed that neither of the ladies at the table had volunteered or been asked to leave while their men "talked business." It was not what he'd have expected had they been in Boston or Philadelphia. But it seemed customs were different here. At least in the home of John Thomas MacKenzie. It made him feel just the least bit uneasy, though he couldn't quite say why.

Possibly it was the girl Rebecca, whose steady gaze never seemed to leave his face. Her expression held the same kind of skeptical curiosity he'd noted on her father's face. Yet she was uncommonly pretty, and he'd willingly have had another sort of conversation with her under different circumstances. But in the present situation . . .

He gave her a friendly smile, which wasn't returned, and then shifted his attention back to MacKenzie. The time had come at last to put forth the proposition he'd traveled all those many miles to present.

"As you perhaps know," he began quietly, "Spain and England are currently at war—though there have been few open hostilities since the Spanish lost their fleet together with the French at Trafalgar."

MacKenzie nodded. Apparently that wasn't news to him.

"The British remain well aware of it, and they haven't forgotten the ceding of Florida back to Spain following the American Revolution. That was an additional blow to their pride, as well as to their hopes for global profit. It seems that now they have plans to undo all of that."

He paused, sitting back to glance at the others around the table. He had everybody's attention at least. But their faces told him nothing.

"From what we believe to be reliable sources in England and elsewhere," he continued, "we have learned they intend to launch an expedition to retake the Floridas some time before the end of this year. Their scheme is to foment an uprising of the Creek Indians against the Spanish and, during that distraction, to land troops at Pensacola. Using that port as a base, they'll then march overland to seize the rest of the colony."

He paused again, and MacKenzie frowned. "They've given no thought," he asked, "to what Mister Bonaparte might say about that?"

"It happens that due to some quirk of diplomacy England and France are not presently at war. And after all the troubles the French have had in the Indies and their recent sale of Louisiana, it seems likely Napoleon has chosen to wash his hands of this hemisphere. Given his present naval weakness," Kirkland shrugged, "there's not very much he can do about it anyway."

After a moment, he frowned and went on: "The consequences of such a seizure for the United States can well be imagined. Britain has never fully lost hope of recovering all her American colonies. A military presence on our southern border could easily lead to further incursions."

He glanced across the table at Jaynes. "That's why we're here. We hope to work secretly to arrange some means of upsetting the British plan."

"Only you two?" Becky's tone was scornful. "If this is of such huge importance to the United States, I'd think your president might send more than a couple of men to take on the entire British Empire!"

Kirkland looked at her and seemed to consider before he continued. "There are a few others who'll join us in St. Augustine. But President Jefferson has made it very clear he intends to keep strict neutrality toward all the European nations. If our mission to Florida should be discovered, he and his government will deny all knowledge of and responsibility for our actions."

He permitted himself a faint smile and a shrug. "That may change in the near future. The president's policy of embargo has proved very unpopular with the public. And there's an election in November."

MacKenzie returned to the subject at hand. "So now that y're here, what is it y've a mind to do? An' even more to the point, what is it has brought y' to come knockin' at my door on this particular evenin'?"

Kirkland turned and met his eyes. "We're hoping that a meeting can be arranged with some of the Creek Indians. If we can convince them an attack on the

Spanish would be contrary to their interests just now, in view of the prospect of well-armed foreign troops overrunning their lands, it could well make the British reconsider their scheme.

"As for why we've come to you"—he spread his hands apart—"we're asking for your help. You've lived in the Floridas for many years, and you know them better than most on our side of their borders. It's reported you're fluent in the native tongue and have generally enjoyed excellent relations with them. If you were to intercede personally to prevent an uprising . . ."

MacKenzie eyed him narrowly and said nothing for several long minutes. There was a frown on his face that came close to a scowl.

"Aye," he said finally. "I have managed to live in peace here in these Floridas for the greater part. Wi' the natives as well as the ones who come from Europe. It is because I mind my own affairs an' let them be to mind theirs. This land we raise our cattle an' crops on is held by their sufferance, an' they know I've no wish to take more of it than I have an' can use." He paused to add pointedly, "Unlike some o' y'r countrymen to the north."

Kirkland nodded. "I'm afraid there's more than a little truth in that, and it's caused no end of trouble on our frontiers. I won't waste time trying to excuse it. Nor will I claim responsibility for it. From what I've heard, the Spanish seem more willing to leave things as they are."

"Aye, they've less hunger for the land. An' scantier resources to seize hold of it, if the truth be told." MacKenzie considered for a moment. "But if the Indians' difficulties are mostly wi' y'r own people, why would they now choose to make war on the Spanish?"

"Trade goods," Sergeant Jaynes said brusquely. "Steel axes, knives, iron cookware, muskets, calico cloth—and rum, of course!"

Kirkland nodded. "As you probably know, the Spanish government has allowed the English firm of John Forbes and Company to keep up their trade monopoly with the Indians since the change of flags. They've resources, capital, and long-established relationships which the Spaniards couldn't match. And we've reports there may also be British agents in that organization whose job is to promote violence by the natives in return for the promise of greater gains. Or, failing that, by threatening to cut off their supply."

MacKenzie nodded. "It could well be," he agreed. "The natives have grown t' rely on the white man's products more an' more, ever since the first o' us arrived on this continent."

"So will you help us?" Kirkland asked frankly. "An Indian war would be at least as devastating to the natives as it would be to the Spanish. Not to mention to the United States."

MacKenzie didn't give his answer right away. He sat frowning in thoughtful silence for what seemed a long time. The Americans watched him with hopeful expectation but knew better than to press their suit any further.

Kirkland glanced at the family around the table. None of them looked at him; their eyes were on their patriarch instead. And none of them had said a word since the lieutenant had first voiced his proposal.

At last MacKenzie stirred himself. His pipe had gone out, and he laid it aside on the surface in front of him.

"No," he said with decision. "No, I will not. I canna' see m'self becomin' involved in y'r affair, either now or in the future. I've no great love for your Mister Jefferson, but the two o' us have this in common: we've both a firm an' lastin' belief in the policy o' strict neutrality."

Kirkland opened his mouth to respond. But the older man wasn't finished.

"I have lived here, as y' say, for a goodly number o' years. Some o' those were under the British Crown an' some were under the Spanish. I've had few troubles with either, or wi' the natives for most o' that time. I've made a home here i' the wilderness for my family an' m'self, an' it is here I mean to abide—simply tendin' to my garden, i' the words o' one very wise man."

There were several seconds of silence. Then Kirkland asked quietly, "Is there nothing more I could say or do that might somehow change your mind?"

"Nothin'." MacKenzie pushed back his chair and made ready to stand up. "I have considered an' reached my decision. It brooks no added discussion."

He got to his feet. "Y're both of y' welcome to sleep i' my house tonight an' break bread wi' us at the dawnin'. But after, we've some cattle to drive to the garrison at St. Augustine. I'll thank you to take y'r leave o' us then. An' not to return."

3

The sun was only a faint gray presence in the east when Kirkland and Sergeant Jaynes came out onto the veranda to greet the new day. There was a brisk chill in the air, but the sky seemed clear and offered promise that the rising sun would bring with it good weather for the driving of cattle and whatever future travels might lie in store for the two of them.

Kirkland breathed deeply and imagined he might just possibly detect a hint of salt on the dank morning air. They were not so very far from the Atlantic Ocean after all. And whether he was deceiving himself or not, it would be a welcome thing to find himself out at sea once again.

Everyone in the MacKenzie household had been awake and stirring about for several hours now, attending to household tasks and preparing for the upcoming journey to St. Augustine. Driving the cattle to the small city would require perhaps a day and a half, including a camp for the night. With time added in for shopping and visiting and what have you, it would likely be three or four days in all before they returned.

Mary MacKenzie would remain behind together with Carlos and Maria to manage things at home. The other employees of the *rancho* were few during the winter months, and they lived in their own cabins some little distance away.

Breakfast after the preparations had mostly been completed was almost as generous a meal as had been dinner the night before. "Breaking bread" for the MacKenzie clan meant fried ham and bacon, *huevos rancheros* (Kirkland had not earlier noticed the chickens but was told they were in a pen behind the house), fresh-baked bread with creamery butter, fruit preserves, and endless quantities of excellent, strong coffee.

Talk around the table revealed the excitement brought on by this rare opportunity for a visit to the only community of any size within hundreds of miles. With a population of three or four thousand, it was the largest in all the Spanish Floridas.

Becky MacKenzie—he'd learned she preferred that name to her father's use of Rebecca—seemed barely able to contain her high spirits while still trying hard not to seem like a child on Christmas morning. But her ready smile and frequent questions about what they might see and do while in the "city" were a clear giveaway.

Kirkland found it difficult not to share her buoyant mood. He stole only occasional glances at her and tried to suppress the smiles her youth and beauty brought unbidden to his lips. It was important that he keep his mind on the task ahead and his serious purpose in Florida.

No one made mention of that purpose during the meal—least of all himself and Sergeant Jaynes. MacKenzie had answered their request for assistance bluntly and definitively the night before. There seemed nothing to gain by taking the risk of antagonizing their host by further testing his resolve.

But as they stood looking on from the veranda while the space before them bustled with activity, saddled horses being brought forth and people scurrying about to make final preparations for the cattle drive, his thoughts remained on his mission. He'd shared none of those thoughts with Sergeant Jaynes as yet. They were still in the formative stage, and there was plenty to occupy his companion's mind with their own upcoming departure and the journey that still lay ahead of them.

He'd watched Jeremiah ride off some minutes before to start the gather of cattle that would be delivered to the Spanish garrison. It would not be a large number, probably no more than some twenty or thirty head.

Below and to his left he saw Mary MacKenzie standing beside the steps in earnest conversation with John Thomas. She was issuing last-minute instructions to her husband about the various items he was to purchase and bring home from the marketplace in St. Augustine.

Those two grown sons of MacKenzie's were an important consideration in the plans he'd now begun forming.

Not too long afterward, he spied Becky MacKenzie as she led her palomino pony around from behind the house. Carlos accompanied her with a bedroll and pack, which he set on the ground nearby when she halted her mount under a tree. He went away to return to the stable, and Kirkland watched while the girl took each of these and stretched up to tie them behind her saddle.

This morning she was wearing a split ankle-length riding dress and a man's woolen shirt under her fringed buckskin jacket. With the broad hat that partly covered her flame-colored hair, she looked every inch the frontier woman he realized she was. And a very handsome sight into the bargain, he thought to himself with a smile that was no longer suppressed.

Carlos reappeared with their own saddled mounts and tied them to the posts in front of the house. Kirkland hardly gave these a glance as he hastily descended the steps and strode across the yard toward Becky.

It had become clear to him that MacKenzie doted on his daughter. Possibly she of all the family could somehow sway his determination to "remain neutral," as he'd called it. In truth, Kirkland had seen little to give him hope this might turn out to be the case. But he thought it was at least worth a try before having to resort to other means.

And if he were completely honest with himself, he'd admit it wasn't the only reason he sought this last opportunity for a few private words with her.

She flashed him a sunny smile as he came close. But the instant he started to broach the subject of his mission again, the smile became a frown, and she shook her head firmly.

"My father is a man who knows his own mind," she said. "He listened to everything you said last night, and after considering it with care he made his decision. Once that was done it may as well have been carved in stone. Neither I nor my brothers, nor even my late mother, I think, could persuade him to alter a particle of it."

Kirkland nodded with resignation. "I was afraid that would be your answer. Still, I wanted to give it one more try."

"The things you said made sense, of course. But then, so did he. And I'm not about to question his judgment."

"I understand. I guess I'll just say good-bye then. I hope you and your family will have a safe journey."

He started to turn away but then stopped and turned back. "I don't suppose," he asked tentatively, "there could be some chance we might meet again in the future?"

"I doubt it." Her voice was neutral, though he wasn't entirely sure the idea hadn't occurred to her. "My father seemed rather definite about that too."

He nodded again and turned to go and rejoin Jaynes, who by this time had untied their horses and mounted his own. He took the reins from the sergeant and stepped up into his saddle. Then both sat and watched while the girl rode off among the trees with her father and brother.

Mary MacKenzie was waving to them from the veranda, and Kirkland lifted a hand in a brief wave of his own. But this was not in imitation of the young wife's farewell. He'd never looked back toward where she stood.

After a moment, Sergeant Jaynes cleared his throat. When there was no response, he cleared it again. It wasn't until after the three riders were completely out of sight that he finally earned a glance from his leader.

"I take it that her answer was no," the older man said. Kirkland nodded. "So what do we do now, Lieutenant?"

Kirkland took up his reins. "We'll ride on to St. Augustine. They're driving cattle, so we'll get there a day or so ahead of them." He clucked to his horse and started it off to the north at a gentle trot. "And once we're there, we'll have a talk with a few of the Spaniards."

After several minutes, when the homestead was out of sight behind them, he slowed his mount to a walk and quietly spoke again. "We still need that man MacKenzie's help. We need it very badly, I think." His hand brushed lightly against the money belt at his waist. "And fortunately, our government has been somewhat more generous with its gold than with its men."

He left the matter there for the present and once more lifted his horse up into a trot.

4

It was market day in St. Augustine. *Vecinos* had come from miles around to offer and seek whatever necessities and small luxuries might be on hand in the colonial capital. The streets and the waterfront plaza were jammed with livestock, carts, and people of all colors and conditions—talking, laughing, haggling, and generally enjoying this opportunity for a welcome break from their daily routines. English, Portuguese, Minorcan, Gullah, and Native American dialects could be heard almost anywhere, as well as the dominant Spanish.

None of this was of any great interest to John Robert and Jeremiah. Once the cattle were sold, they'd used a portion of the proceeds for the purchases ordered by Mary MacKenzie and then were anxious to set out again for what they'd planned as an extended return journey to the homestead. They would spend several days hunting and camping along the way, among the quieter and less crowded woodlands that each preferred. They bid their father and sister a cheerful farewell and wasted no time leaving the bustle of "city life" behind.

Becky, for her part, had not the slightest intention of abandoning these colorful surroundings just yet. Like any young woman who spent almost all her days in near isolation, she was irresistibly drawn to the diverse collection of sights and sounds that assailed her from every direction—and, of course, to the rare opportunity to do a bit of shopping.

Her father, his purse now comfortably heavy with the Spanish *reales* he'd gotten for the cattle, was more than happy to keep her company. He wasn't opposed to a break from daily routines as well. There were friends and acquaintances here whom he hadn't seen for a number of months. And perhaps he might even find it in himself to make a few small purchases of his own.

The two had just enjoyed a pleasant lunch at a Spanish *posada* and were taking a leisurely stroll along the quay when they were approached by two uniformed Spanish soldiers. Close behind them was an officer, who spoke as soon as he came near.

"*¿Señor Juan Tomás MacKenzie?*"

"Aye—*si*." MacKenzie looked at the officer.

"I have received orders for your arrest, *Señor*."

"My arrest? For what? What possible charge might y' be bringin' against me?"

"I regret that this has not been confided to me, *Señor*. Only that you are to be disarmed and confined in the *Castillo*"—he gave a slight shrug—"temporarily."

"But that's nonsense!" There were spots of color on Becky's cheeks as she glared at the young officer. "My father has lived here for years and everybody knows him! There's not a more law-abiding man in all of the Floridas!"

She knew as well as MacKenzie—and the officer—that "temporarily" could mean anything from an hour or two to decades in a Spanish prison. The English principle of habeas corpus was not a part of Spanish jurisprudence.

"Nevertheless, *Señorita*," the officer told her calmly, "I have my orders." He turned to MacKenzie. "Will you come peacefully, *Señor*? I am instructed to use force if required."

Becky was about to launch into another furious outburst but was restrained by her father's gentle hand upon her arm.

"I will come with y' willin'ly," he said to the officer. "Yet I would deem it a courtesy if y'd inform Governor Enrique White o' this matter. I canna' doubt but that there's been some unaccountable mistake made."

He carefully removed the pistol and large sheathed knife from his belt and handed them to his daughter. As she reached out to take them, she happened to glance beyond him and see Lieutenant Kirkland and Sergeant Jaynes standing among the small group of onlookers. Their presence here at this moment struck her as a curious coincidence.

When she returned her attention to her father, he was gazing seriously down into her face. "I trust y' will keep y'r wits about y' now, young lady, an' make no difficulty for the authorities. If y've heard no word o' me by this evenin', y've my leave to call upon the governor y'rself in order to inquire. But I've small doubt 't will all be resolved before then."

She nodded without replying, then stood and watched while he turned with a soldier at either side and strode off in the direction of the massive gray walls of the *Castillo*. When she finally looked back, the onlookers had dispersed, and the Americans had disappeared.

She was alone now on the quay and had no idea of what to do next. She looked behind her in the direction of the busy marketplace and felt a helpless sense of anger and frustration. Her earlier lighthearted notions of shopping and sightseeing in the colonial capital seemed trivial now and even a little bit childish. There were far more serious matters to be considered at present.

But then what could be done? What could *she* do?

She wasn't prepared to accept her father's optimistic assurance that "'t will all be resolved" before nightfall. In fact, knowing him as she did, she doubted his words expressed his personal convictions so much as an attempt to ease her own worries about him.

In which case, they hadn't succeeded.

Well, practical things first. There were the two horses that had brought them here to St. Augustine, along with their packs and other gear. These they had left outside the *posada* where they'd had lunch, with plans to recover them after no more than an hour or so.

It could be a much longer time now before they were needed. Perhaps not until tomorrow. Or perhaps . . . She forced that unwanted thought aside for the present.

She went to fetch the horses and led them to a livery stable her father had pointed out to her a few blocks from the square. She'd a small number of gold *reales* her father had given her, and she presented one to the hostler with a promise of more if the animals' stay should prove a long one. The old Spaniard was pleased enough to accept this offer, as well as her promise. Gold was a rare thing in Florida these days.

She debated with herself for a minute or so about what to do with the pistol she'd been handed and decided to conceal it in the packs she left with the horses. The single-shot weapon wasn't likely to be of much use to her here in the city, and the sight of a young woman so armed could cause unwanted comment. Not being any more trusting than good sense might suggest, she waited until the hostler's back was turned before shoving the firearm between some blankets.

This immediate task completed, she left the stable thinking about where to go next. It seemed that the only hope of freeing her father must lie with the Spanish authorities. And ultimately this meant the colony's governor. Her father had given her permission to go see him. But not until evening.

She glanced up at the sun. It was now several hours past noon. Try as she might, she couldn't come up with any helpful ideas about how she might spend the intervening hours. And the thought of idly doing nothing for all that time was more than she could bear.

"Evening," she decided at last, could always be somewhat loosely interpreted. And in the present circumstances . . . She squared her shoulders and directed her steps toward the governor's residence at one end of the square.

The *functionario* who greeted her inside the entrance was polite and officious. But in the manner of all bureaucrats everywhere, he had little help to offer.

"I regret, *Señorita*, that Governor White is not present in the city today. He may be expected to return tomorrow. Or perhaps the day after."

Was there anyone else here in the government offices that could help with a legal matter? Regrettably, no. Anyone she might speak with who could at least tell her what charges had been brought against her father? Alas, *lo siento*.

Becky thanked him briefly and left, swallowing the angry tirade that was making every effort to burst forth.

She crossed the square to the waterfront in a dark mood of helpless rage and frustration. There seemed nowhere she could turn to find anything at all that might aid her father. The tempting sights and clamor of the marketplace were scarcely even noticed now, no longer playing any part in her plans.

For a time she stood and gazed out across the shimmering waters of Matanzas Inlet, thinking gloomy thoughts when she permitted herself any thoughts at all. Then, for lack of something better to do, she walked along the quay until she came to a square mooring stone some hundred yards distant from the looming *Castillo*.

She sat there and simply stared at its massive gray walls, thinking that, if nothing else, she might at least feel closer to her father this way—despite being utterly unable to improve his plight.

It came to her after a while that with all of her walking here and there about the small city, she hadn't once set eyes on Lieutenant Kirkland and his sergeant again. Not since that single brief glimpse at the moment her father was arrested.

She wondered if there was any possibility that she might ever see them again.

5

The cell inside the thick coquina walls of the *Castillo* was dark, chill, and musty-smelling. A single narrow window some ten feet above the stone floor afforded the only light once the heavy, iron-bound door had thudded shut at MacKenzie's back.

The afternoon sun outside had been bright, and at first he could make out almost nothing of his surroundings. He stood where he was for several long minutes to let his eyes adjust to the dark. After the booted footsteps of the soldiers who'd brought him faded away, he heard a few faint scuffling noises from across the cell. Rats?

Finally his eyes caught a movement on the floor underneath the window. Much larger than any rat. A shadowy figure slowly unfolded itself and rose from the place where it had been seated against the wall. It took a few wary steps closer, then stopped and thrust its head forward as if examining the newcomer suspiciously.

After several seconds there was a sharp intake of breath, and the figure moved even closer. There was a moment or two of silence.

"MacKenzie?" The figure made a slow half circle around the new arrival, still studying him intently. "B' God, I do believe it is no other!"

The man who'd spoken stepped back a little and shook his head. "The years have been kind to you, my boyo. Though t' be sure they have left their mark. As is no doubt the case wi' each of us."

The mocking Irish lilt was familiar, though it had been two decades since MacKenzie last heard it. Even in the dim light he felt sure he recognized the speaker.

"James Tyrone," he said quietly, "unless I am very much mistaken."

The man in front of him took another step back and made a sweeping sardonic bow. "At your service. 'T would seem that fate has finally brought us together again after all these long years apart!"

MacKenzie watched in silence while his cellmate came erect and his voice took on a harsh edge. "An' with never a weapon to hand when it's needed, here in this foul dark coffin o' stone!"

His bitterness wasn't surprising. It was MacKenzie who'd personally brought about the man's downfall when these Florida colonies were English.

That was almost thirty years ago, and "Dread Jamie Tyrone"—a onetime pirate, deadly swordsman, and ruthless seeker of political power—had had a well-earned reputation as a dangerous foe. They'd fought each other in those days long past, and MacKenzie had won the decision.* Afterward he'd managed to seize a cache of his enemy's pirate gold. It was this money that he'd used to establish his prosperous *rancho* here in the Floridas.

When the fighting was over, he'd turned the other man loose, against his better judgment and realizing he'd made a deadly enemy. But he'd not been so ruthless as to kill even Tyrone in cold blood. Instead, he'd offered him at least the slim possibility of surviving a solitary trek through the dangerous swamps and untracked wilderness of East Florida.

There had been no word of him at all in the Floridas since that time. Yet here at last was proof that he'd somehow managed to make good his escape. Where he might have been during the interim MacKenzie could hardly guess. But he'd little reason to believe the Irish rogue would have changed his ways. And it was clear that his thirst for revenge had not grown any less over the years.

MacKenzie's muscles tensed, half expecting an assault. Yet he was not greatly worried about such an eventuality. He was a good head taller than the man now before him, and he still had much the same strength he'd had as a youth. The only possible danger might lie in the future, if their imprisonment together should prove a long one. He must guard against any careless lapse of attention or a tendency to drowse.

Tyrone confirmed his judgment, turning with an exaggerated show of indifference and retracing his steps across the cell to take his former seat by the far wall.

MacKenzie sat down in his turn, with his back against the rough coquina surface next to the entrance. He made himself as comfortable as possible on the

---

*As recounted in *Trail from St. Augustine* by Lee Gramling (1993).

cold stone floor, his eyes never straying from the huddled form of his enemy. He'd little doubt that Tyrone's attention was fixed on him as well.

Neither of them spoke again for what seemed a long time. But then Tyrone, who'd always impressed MacKenzie as a bit of a compulsive talker, shifted his position slightly and finally broke the silence.

"An' now what could it be, I'm wonderin', that might bring an upstanding citizen like yourself into this sorry state—compelled wi' me to share the harsh confines o' this humble abode?"

MacKenzie didn't answer for several seconds. But then he decided there could be little harm in talking to the man. It would serve to pass the time, and he might even learn something useful from his fellow prisoner.

"I' truth," he said with a shrug, "I've no idea. The *teniente* who brought me here said little, an' I believe he had no more knowledge o' the matter than m'self. I've hopes there will be further word sometime today. Or at worst upon the morrow."

Tyrone didn't respond, and after a few moments MacKenzie asked in his turn, "An' yourself?" His curiosity was genuine, but he made it sound as if he was simply making idle conversation.

"A mere accident o' the times," Tyrone answered with a shrug of his own. "It seems our neighbors to the north, since the first o' this year, have made it a law forbiddin' the import o' slaves to their country. I'd a goodly cargo o' black-birds on board my schooner the *Raven* when one o' their cutters appeared outside the bar here an' commanded us to heave to. Before we'd an opportunity to discuss the matter, a Spanish vessel arrived alongside an' claimed the capture for themselves."

He paused and muttered a curse. "They coveted my ship a great deal more than her cargo, I think. An' now 't will cost me a pretty penny in bribes if ever I'm to resolve the business!"

MacKenzie nodded in silence. Trafficking in slaves was what he might have expected from Tyrone. No doubt safer than piracy and very likely more profitable.

There were a few minutes more of desultory conversation before each of them fell silent again, and the long afternoon wore on. The hours seemed to pass with agonizing slowness. No word arrived from the Spanish about the charges against MacKenzie, nor were there any other communications from their jailors.

Gradually the light outside the high window began fading to gray, and after a long while MacKenzie grew drowsy in spite of himself. He let his eyes close for only a moment—

And jerked them open again with a start to find the dark form of Tyrone looming over him. Somewhere in the cell the Irishman had laid hands on a short length of chain and now was in the process of swinging it back to send it crashing down on his enemy's head.

MacKenzie's left hand shot out, and he seized the other man's wrist in a grip of steel. Tyrone let out a yelp of pain as the sharp twist that followed loosened his hold on the chain and sent it rattling to the floor.

Without loosening his grip, MacKenzie rose to his feet and drew back his right fist to deliver a crushing blow. But in that instant there was the sound of the heavy bolt being removed from the door behind him. He hesitated briefly and turned his head to glance over his shoulder as the iron-bound portal swung ponderously open.

Tyrone seized upon this distraction to wrench himself free and scurry across the cell, where he'd be temporarily out of reach. MacKenzie cursed softly at his escape but was still dividing his attention between his enemy and the entrance.

From the darkling shadows outside in the corridor, both men now heard a drunken tenor voice uplifted in song:

"Tim Finnegan lived in Wattlin' Street, a gentle Irishman mighty odd . . ."

6

Two soldiers appeared in the opening, each holding onto the arm of an unsteady and bedraggled figure. Without a word they shoved the man roughly inside and closed the door behind him. MacKenzie heard the heavy bolt drop back into place.

Tyrone remained standing with his back against the far wall, his eyes shifting from his old enemy to the new arrival and back again. For a minute or two MacKenzie studied their new cellmate in the fading light from the high window.

His clothes were patched and more than a little askew, and they appeared to contain some worn articles of military dress. He wasn't as tall as either of his fellow prisoners but appeared to be wiry and of muscular build with a nut-brown face that spoke of years spent in the out-of-doors. Yet he wasn't a young man. His tangled mop of hair, once dark, showed streaks of gray.

He seemed to take no notice of this curious scrutiny. Assuming a wobbly pose near the center of the cell, he threw back his head and went on with his song.

"He'd a beautiful brogue so rich and sweet. To rise in the world he carried a hod.

"Y'see he'd a sort of a tipplin' way, with a love for the liquor poor Tim was born . . ."

At this point the newcomer seemed to become aware of his two cellmates for the first time. He paused, looked from one to the other, grinned, and laid a finger beside his nose.

"A half a man with his work each day an' a drop o' the craythur every morn . . ."

Then he broke off and made an unsteady bow.

"Gentlemen, I believe introductions are in order. My name is Michael Patrick O'Shaughnessy, late of his Spanish Catholic Majesty's Hibernia Regiment. An' you, my two companions in misfortune, would be?"

MacKenzie and Tyrone each gave their names, still eying one another with wary hostility. O'Shaughnessy seemed unaware of the tension between them.

"A very great honor, I'm sure." He attempted an even deeper bow, which wound up costing him his precarious equilibrium. He plopped down cross-legged on the floor between them.

"The curse of the craythur it is," he confessed sadly with a shake of his head. "An' no mistakin'. But then what's a lad to do? Thirty years with the auld regiment, man an' boy. Then t' be cast off like some ill-used pick an' wisk wi' naught but a pittance to keep body an' soul together." He sounded almost on the verge of tears.

The others in the cell offered no response, and none seemed expected. The old soldier wasn't looking at them and now appeared lost in his memories of the past.

"Ah, what a grand sight it was, that day we stormed the Queen's Redoubt before Pensacola! It was Arturo O'Neill himself led the charge, he that was after governor o' these Floridas. An' all the brave lads let out a great shout an' followed close behind, myself included."

He went rambling on about the West Florida campaign, as if he were speaking only to himself. After a few moments, MacKenzie paid him little attention. He leaned back against the coquina wall and kept his eyes constantly on the shadowed form of Tyrone. This time he was grimly determined to stay awake.

Yet, for now at least, his enemy seemed to have abandoned any hostile plans. He resumed his seat on the stone floor and folded his arms, then lowered his head upon them. A less suspicious man than MacKenzie might have thought him asleep.

O'Shaughnessy droned on as the light outside the window grew darker. He expanded his reminiscences to include other events of his military career in Cuba, Spain, and elsewhere. His rambling narrative seemed endless, and the hours crept slowly past.

At last the cell was cloaked in inky blackness. MacKenzie was more alert than ever now. His sharpened senses reached out to catch any faint sound of movement that might come from behind the speaker, from the place he'd last seen Tyrone. For a long time there was nothing.

Then he could hear sounds behind him. There was a stealthy scuffing of feet in the passage outside the cell. This was followed moments later by the rasp of the heavy bolt being lifted. MacKenzie frowned and shifted his attention toward the entrance. It was fully night by now and very late.

The door swung back to reveal the yellow glow from a shielded lantern. In its dim light stood two men. Each held a cocked pistol in his hand.

With a start of surprise, MacKenzie recognized the shadowy figures. They were the same ones who'd spent the night in his home two days ago.

"Outside, you two. You're coming with us." Lieutenant Kirkland stepped a little aside and gestured with his pistol.

Sergeant Jaynes was behind him holding the lantern. And the weapon in his other hand never wavered.

For a long moment no one inside the cell moved or made a sound. Then MacKenzie found his voice.

"What is it now that brings the two of y' here to the *Castillo* at this late hour? An' what would be the meanin' o' those weapons?"

"It means you're being released from this place into our custody." There was a faint smile on Kirkland's face. "Without the benefit of official sanction. And tonight we'll all be taking our leave of St. Augustine."

He paused, and the smile disappeared. "Or would you rather spend the rest of your days in a Spanish prison on the charges of smuggling and crimes against the state?"

"I am guilty of neither, as is very well known."

"There's a certain quantity of American gold that says otherwise. And as usual, the Spanish *situado* is late in arriving."

"I see." MacKenzie nodded with understanding. "Y've paid y'r thirty pieces o' silver to the Spaniards so y' can seize me an' take me off with y'."

"It's gold, actually. But not everyone has received the benefit of our generosity. So it's vital we move quickly now." He gestured again with his pistol. "Step lively. There's a boat waiting, and we mean to be well out to sea before daylight."

He lifted his voice slightly and called into the darkness beyond MacKenzie. "You too! We'll leave no one behind who could report what's happened!"

Tyrone got to his feet and came forward. "I will accompany you an' gladly. I find I have no great love for the Spaniard's hospitality."

It took O'Shaughnessy a bit longer to struggle up and appear in the lamplight.

"Wait. Who's this?" Kirkland looked quickly from one to the other of the two Irishmen. "We were told there were only two."

Tyrone smiled and waved a hand at their recent companion. "Mister O'Shaughnessy joined us last evening. Drunk an' disorderly I believe was the charge."

"Wi' a small bit o' discreet smugglin'," the other informed him with dignity.

"Well . . ." Kirkland scowled and then shrugged. "All right. You'll have to come too." He made room at the entrance. "Single file now, the three of you. Out into the passage and then to the gate. We'll be behind you every step, so don't do anything foolish."

MacKenzie let the others go first, but he followed along without complaint. It seemed he'd no other choice under the circumstances. At least until he could think of some worthwhile plan.

Kirkland and Jaynes hurried the men at gunpoint out through the conveniently abandoned entrance to the *Castillo*, across the bridge over its dry moat, and past the ravelin. From there they were directed down a slope to the nearby water's edge.

A black-painted longboat awaited them with six men seated at the oars. They were Americans, it seemed, from what could be heard of their whispered words.

No delay was brooked in getting aboard, and in minutes the sailors were pulling strongly through the dark waters of the inlet. By the light from a partial moon, MacKenzie could make out the silhouette of a sleek two-masted schooner before them in the near distance.

Their oars had been muffled, but they made enough noise to cover any small sound from the shallows behind them. The rowers were bent to their task, and no one else thought to look back to see the strong, slim hand that rose up from the surface and gripped the boat's trailing painter.

7

There could not be much doubt that the schooner was their destination. No other vessels were anchored nearby, and Kirkland, who was at the helm, was steering directly for it.

This was clear to Tyrone as well. He muttered a sharp curse and tried to rise to his feet in the crowded boat. "That's my ship, b'God! It's my schooner, the *Raven!*"

Sergeant Jaynes clamped a hand on his shoulder and held him down. The pistol in his other hand came up to touch Tyrone's cheek. "Be still!" he commanded in a harsh whisper.

"It is the *Raven,*" Kirkland confirmed softly. "Although there's a small question of ownership at present. The Spanish have seized it as contraband together with its cargo."

"They lost no time takin' my cargo ashore," Tyrone said bitterly. "But 's far as I know I've still my crewmen aboard."

"Two of them," the American answered calmly. "Or so we've been told. Along with a Spanish guard."

As they drew alongside, the rowers shipped their oars, and everyone's eyes were drawn to the moonlit deck above them, watching it sharply for any signs of activity. Kirkland gave out a low-pitched whistle.

Tyrone, with a strong suspicion of what was afoot, shoved Jaynes's pistol aside and ducked under his grip. He twisted away and stood up in the boat, opening his mouth to shout a warning to his crew.

But before the words could leave his lips, he was enfolded by the flailing arms of the drunken Michael O'Shaughnessy, who'd apparently chosen to lurch to his feet at the very same moment. They collapsed together between the thwarts and were roughly seized and silenced by the nearest American sailors.

Kirkland glanced impatiently at the melee and then returned his eyes to the schooner's deck. A man in Spanish uniform had appeared at the rail. He peered down into the longboat and nodded in recognition. A moment later he'd thrown a rope ladder over the side and wordlessly turned away to vanish again from sight.

Without pausing for a second Kirkland leapt to the ladder and started clambering up it hand over hand. Four of the sailors followed instantly, leaving Jaynes and the other two behind to watch over their prisoners.

The boarding party swiftly vaulted the rail, and for some several minutes no one in the boat saw or heard anything further.

Then there was the noise of a pair of brief scuffles fore and aft. A few angry cries were stilled almost instantly by what had the sound of heavy blows. And again there was silence.

Before very long Kirkland reappeared at the rail. "The rest of you can come on board now," he called down to them. "The vessel is ours."

When he'd gained his footing on the deck, MacKenzie could see that a staysail had been set at the bow, and he heard the sounds of the anchor being weighed.

Tyrone was cursing furiously several feet away, every ounce of his considerable venom directed at the young lieutenant who stood calmly nearby overseeing the activities.

"What in the bloody blazes do y' think you're about now, seizin' my vessel like some thrice-damned filibuster in the dark o' the night?" The irony of his choice of words seemed lost on the former pirate. "I've more than a little mind to—"

His tirade was cut short by two loud splashes from somewhere astern.

"It seems," Kirkland said quietly, "that your men have just abandoned your ship, Captain Tyrone. And I have taken her into service for the United States Navy." He favored the other with a wry smile. "She is, as you know, a good fast sailor. And her shallow draft will also serve us well in these Florida waters."

Any further protest or physical response from the *Raven*'s former owner was forestalled by the glowering approach of Sergeant Jaynes, who still held the cocked pistol in his fist. Tyrone turned and stomped angrily off toward the bow, still grumbling curses under his breath.

Two of the sailors jumped back into the longboat to bring it around and place it in tow. Kirkland strode to the helm and took hold of the wheel. In a matter of minutes the *Raven* was gliding smoothly over the bar, leaving the small harbor of St. Augustine behind.

Before swinging her bow out into the broad waters of the Atlantic, however, they first made their way south, hugging the sandy coast of Anastasia Island. MacKenzie wondered at the reason for this, but it was not very long before it became clear.

The Spanish soldier, whom he'd momentarily forgotten, now reappeared and came to stand before Kirkland. The American took a small purse from his belt and held it out to the man, who quickly made it disappear somewhere about his person.

The soldier gave a sly grin and leaned forward to expose his chin, letting Kirkland deal him a single sharp blow that was calculated to raise a livid bruise but cause no serious damage.

One of the sailors threw some water on his face, and as soon as the Spaniard recovered sufficiently to be helped to his feet, he made his way across to the starboard rail. He gripped it and gazed off for a moment toward the moonlit sands and the dark silhouettes of palm trees a few hundred yards distant. Then, raising his hand in a sardonic salute, he swung his legs over and leaped out into the water.

Kirkland instantly called for more canvas to be laid on and began to spin the wheel. The schooner heeled over to point her bow southeast into the wide moonlit expanse of the Atlantic.

MacKenzie had been watching all these events from a short distance away. Now he moved closer to where Kirkland stood at the helm.

"West Florida?" he said quietly when the two of them were alone.

"West Florida," the younger man confirmed. "The Apalachicola River, to be exact. It's navigable for quite some distance upstream, which ought to bring us close to the Indian villages where we will hope to meet with the Creeks."

"An' what might it be y're supposin' to do then? I've made it clear enough to y' that I'll have no part in y'r affairs between nations."

Kirkland glanced at him and shrugged. "It will take us a week or so to round the peninsula and reach the Apalachicola. That should give us both plenty of time to get better acquainted." He smiled.

"Who knows? It may be you'll reconsider."

8

The sun hung over the eastern horizon in a brilliant cloudless sky when MacKenzie left the small ship's cabin he'd been assigned and came out onto the deck. He'd slept later than usual after the events of the previous night. But in truth there was little he could think of to do in his present situation that would justify an early rising.

Since Kirkland's actions had left little doubt he was now the Americans' prisoner, he'd been somewhat surprised to find his cabin door unlocked and no guard nearby to watch it. But a glance to the west made the reason clear enough. There was nothing to see in that direction but long, rolling blue-green swells.

When he thought about it, he recalled that he'd felt a certain amount of turbulence during the night. Not so much as to suggest a storm but what might be expected from a crossing of the Gulf Stream. The schooner's course was due south at the moment, and that strong north-moving current came very near to the Florida coast in places. Running outside it made for a faster voyage on their way to round the peninsula. But it also meant that by this morning they must be many watery miles from land.

There was no question that the young naval lieutenant meant to arrive at his destination without the slightest delay. Every bit of canvas the ship would bear now billowed from the masts and stays, drawing well in a fresh northeasterly breeze. He could hear the swish of the schooner's bow as it sliced its way through the waves.

"A good morning to you, Mister MacKenzie!" Kirkland handed the wheel over to a sailor and stepped down from his place at the helm. Today he was wearing his naval uniform. "I trust you've slept well."

MacKenzie looked at him narrowly for a moment. But then he shrugged. The man had greeted him courteously enough. Almost as if he were now a guest on his ship. There was nothing to be gained by repaying such courtesy with angry words.

"Well enough," he replied. "It's been some number o' years since I've found m'self at sea. But after y've made y'r peace wi' the rollin', there's naught can be more restful."

"I agree completely. And I'm pleased to hear you're a good sailor." He came closer and reached out a hand. After a brief hesitation, MacKenzie took it.

"Breakfast?" his host and captor suggested with a smile.

"I believe I may manage that. Since I've now made my peace wi' the rollin'."

"Then let's go below together and see what we can find." Kirkland led the way down a short series of steps into the schooner's main salon. "I've already eaten, but I'll join you for coffee. I hope you like it strong and black."

"There's no other kind, I'm thinkin'."

MacKenzie took a seat at the built-in table while Kirkland went past him into the ship's small galley. He spoke over his shoulder. "We're a little short-handed here, as you might imagine. So I'll play the part of steward."

He returned after a few minutes with two steaming mugs and a pewter plate filled with food. "Cold roast fowl, fresh fruit, and buttered bread—courtesy of the former Captain Tyrone's most recent landfall. The salt pork and hardtack will wait for another time."

MacKenzie tasted the coffee, grunted approval, and set about the meal with a will. His plans for a good supper at the Spanish *posada* the previous night had been curtailed by his unwanted imprisonment.

"Speakin' o' Mister Tyrone," he said between bites, "where might the man be at the present?"

"Confined in a cabin forward." Kirkland sat on the bench across from him. "He's a rather violent temper, as I guess you saw. And as I said, we're a little short-handed." He took a sip of coffee and shrugged. "I'd gladly have left him to cool his heels back there in the *Castillo* if I didn't think he'd report to the authorities. Or to some British spy he might have knowledge of."

"Aye. 'T would be likely." MacKenzie continued to eat for a minute; then he took another swallow of coffee. "An' what o' the other . . . gentleman . . . who came on board wi' us?"

"Mister O'Shaughnessy has been the soul of cooperation thus far." Kirkland grinned. "Encouraged by a small tot of rum now and then from the stores Tyrone had aboard."

MacKenzie finished his meal without further questions. Kirkland replenished their coffee and returned to his seat. After a minute or two, he started to speak casually of himself, his New England beginnings, and his naval career.

MacKenzie listened at first with little interest. He'd no place to go and nothing he needed to do, so if the man wanted to talk, he was pleased enough to just sit there in comfort and let him ramble on.

But as the narrative continued through several refills of coffee, he realized there was more to it than a simple idling away of the time. The American meant to provide enough information about himself to create some kind of common ground between them. His manner made it clear he wasn't seeking the older man's approval or friendship—only a better understanding of who he was and what it was that moved him to act in the ways he did.

And as he talked on, MacKenzie started to find himself interested in spite of himself. For a man of his relative youth, Kirkland had led an eventful life. Like many others born to seafaring families, he'd shipped out aboard a fishing vessel before he reached his teens. Later he'd joined the navy, serving at first on the schooner *Enterprise* in America's undeclared war against the French. Then, after a promotion to ensign, he'd sailed with the frigate *Constellation* on its mission to face the Barbary pirates.

MacKenzie had heard stories of both conflicts, and he realized that if nothing else, the man with him was an experienced sailor and a proven fighting man. He had to admit he was impressed. He'd done a bit of fighting himself in his younger years, though never in any organized conflict between nations. There was a kind a of unspoken bond between all men who'd faced an armed enemy in battle.

As it happened, Kirkland's associate, Sergeant Jaynes, could lay claim to combat honors as well. During the Barbary War he'd been on the famous trek through the North African desert to seize the town of Derna.

In time the younger man shifted the talk to questions about MacKenzie's own life and background. To these he said little. He'd always preferred to "let the dead past bury its dead," as the saying went. Even in the case of the recent and unwelcome reappearance of a very much alive "Dread Jamie Tyrone."

He did admit to being born and coming of age in the then British colony of South Carolina. But at eighteen he'd left there to seek his fortune in Florida. And he made it clear that he felt no special loyalty to his birthplace, under either its past or its present government.

Nor to the king of Spain or his New World empire, in point of fact. His only true allegiance was to his sons and daughter and to the *rancho* that was their home and livelihood. These he would defend to the death. But as for any earthly nation or government, he simply accepted these as necessary evils and did what he had to do to keep the peace and preserve what was his.

Kirkland told him that he understood, though his own views were somewhat different.

It didn't escape MacKenzie's notice that during all their long conversation, the young lieutenant never made mention of his present purpose in Florida or his earlier request for help. It was a subject that neither had forgotten; yet it was clear that Kirkland could be a patient and calculating man.

The kind that would bear some careful watching.

In time they both fell silent, and before very long, there was a hail from one of the men on deck requesting the captain's presence. Kirkland got up and took his leave, saying as he did that he hoped his "guest's" stay aboard ship would be a comfortable one.

MacKenzie thanked him and stayed where he was, thinking about all that was said and what he had learned. Despite his stubborn resolve not to yield to any sort of blandishment, he'd found himself almost starting to like the fellow. They did seem to have a good bit in common.

It was a little as if—he scowled at the thought—the other man might have been a younger version of himself.

9

After a while, left to his own devices and with apparent freedom of the ship, MacKenzie returned their dishes to the galley and went up on deck.

He'd only seen the schooner's outline in darkness and not much else since coming aboard. He was curious and decided to take a turn about the deck to learn something more of his new home—or his prison.

She was a fair-sized vessel, perhaps a hundred feet in length but much narrower at the waist. At the stern, where he began his tour, there was a low superstructure with the ship's wheel and binnacle on top and steps leading up on either side. The front of the superstructure contained the hatchway that led down to the salon. It was flanked by two narrower doors, one of which opened to his own small cabin. The other, he guessed, would be the cabin occupied by Kirkland.

In the center of the ship, between the two masts, was a single large hold that had earlier held the slaves Tyrone was transporting. The hatch covers had been pulled off now, and the smell from its depths was strong and unpleasant—mute testimony to the conditions its chained human cargo had been forced to endure.

Toward the bow was another low superstructure, with doors facing aft that matched the ones at the stern. The space on its top was occupied by two canvas-covered boats, each a bit larger than the pair of lifeboats he passed along the rail opposite the hold.

As he continued his way forward, MacKenzie met a sailor who'd just emerged from the central opening in front of him. When asked, the man explained that this led down some steps to the crew's quarters, where there were hammocks instead of bunks. The cabin on the left was the one where Tyrone was confined, and the other had been taken by Sergeant Jaynes. O'Shaughnessy, he was told, slept with the crew.

Though the cabin he'd spent the night in was tiny by most standards, Mac-Kenzie realized he was privileged to have been awarded one at all. It seemed he was to be treated more like an honored guest aboard the schooner than a prisoner.

Which didn't make his unwilling presence here any less disagreeable.

The deck narrowed beyond the forward superstructure and continued on around the bow. MacKenzie completed this circuit and made his way aft again toward the place where he'd begun.

Then he found a solitary place at the rail and stood there for a long time gazing out across the featureless sea, taking in deep breaths of the fresh salt air and giving himself up to the mindless sensations of wind in his face and motion under his feet.

He wasted no thought on the future and little on his present situation. There wasn't very much he could do about either at the moment. When a time came for action, as he felt sure it would sooner or later, he'd make what decisions were needed then and carry them through without hesitation.

After a while he turned and rested his back against the rail, watching while the sailors managed the sails and went about making the *Raven* shipshape. A couple of them had been given the unpleasant task of swamping out the hold. The fact that these men could be seen frequently raising their heads above deck to take in large gulps of the fresh air attested to its former state.

Suddenly there was a cry from above, and every man in the crew interrupted whatever he was doing to start shifting the booms and hauling on the sheets. The wind had made a turn to the southwest, and the schooner was having to tack and continue on a close reach in order to keep to its southerly course.

As he watched all the activity, MacKenzie spied Michael O'Shaughnessy weaving unsteadily along the narrow deck beside the hold. He seemed blithely unaware of the risk of being swept overboard by each swing of a boom. Yet somehow, as he made his wobbly way forward, he was miraculously able to avoid this—at times by what seemed scarcely a hair's breadth.

MacKenzie scowled and shook his head. Luck of the Irish, he thought. Or of the habitual drunkard. The man was a danger both to himself and to others. It would be far better if he were to be put ashore to fend for himself. But of course there was no possibility of that until they finally made landfall, some days ahead in thinly populated West Florida.

The rest of the afternoon passed uneventfully, punctuated only by occasional shouts and muffled curses from the locked forward compartment that housed James Tyrone.

Toward evening the wind changed again, bringing with it choppy seas and periodic squalls of rain. With a hat and slicker borrowed from the ship's stores, MacKenzie was content to remain on deck. His spacious home in East Florida was a pleasure and a comfort to him, but he'd never completely lost his love for the out-of-doors. And his quarters on the *Raven* were not at all spacious. To him their dark and spartan interior seemed little better than the Spanish prison.

While he stood watching rain and spindrifts chase each other across the deck, his attention was drawn to the tarpaulin-covered lifeboat at the starboard rail. O'Shaughnessy was bending over it, and he seemed to be exchanging heated words with another person. The Irishman had undone some of the cover's lashings to lift up a corner, and his harangue appeared directed at someone inside the boat.

The wind made his words impossible to catch, and MacKenzie started making his way forward over the rolling deck out of a mixture of curiosity and concern. At a sound behind him, he glanced back and saw Kirkland had noticed the commotion as well. He'd turned the helm over to one of his crew and was coming to investigate the trouble for himself.

When he got close enough to be heard, MacKenzie called out, "What is it, man? Have y' discovered a stowaway in yon boat?"

O'Shaughnessy turned around with his fists on his hips. "I have that." There was a scowl on his face, and he shook his head. "An' a glorious mess she has made of it too!"

"She?" MacKenzie came closer while O'Shaughnessy bent to untie more of the tarp and throw it aside.

The occupant of the boat struggled awkwardly up to a sitting position, a rueful smile on her pale, greenish face. "Hello, Father. I'm afraid I wasn't cut out for the life of a sailor!"

"Rebecca!"

The smile gave way to a sickly grimace. "You know I've never been at sea before. And right now I don't think I ever want to be again!"

The rain streaked down her face and dripped from flaccid tendrils of auburn hair. Her clothes were stained and sodden as a result of both storm and seasickness. Nor was the smell that arose from the small boat even remotely what anyone could call ladylike.

It was an apparition that only a father could love. And MacKenzie wasn't so very sure about that at the moment.

"What in the blue blazes are y' doin' on this ship?"

"I followed you." Her shrug suggested that no further explanation should be needed. "Do you suppose you could find me a wet cloth or something I can use to clean up a bit?"

"What in the . . . ?" This was Kirkland, who'd arrived to stand next to Mac-Kenzie with a glowering scowl on his face.

"Good evening, Lieutenant." Becky sat up straighter and addressed him as sedately as possible under the circumstances. "You once took advantage of our hospitality. Now I've come aboard ship to share yours."

Kirkland turned his scowl on MacKenzie. "Is everybody in your family completely crazy?! Or is it only the two of you?!"

"I'd always believed m' self o' sound enough mind." The older man shook his head. "But now here wi' my daughter, I am beginnin' to wonder." He glanced at the girl in the boat, then met Kirkland's eyes. "I will tell you this much though: whenever Rebecca has taken it into her head to do a thing, it is a foolish man would make shift to say her nay."

"You've never forbidden her to do anything at all?"

"I have, for what small good it's done me. A man may keep his senses and still be a fool."

"Now let's be honest." Becky looked at her father. "You never told me not to keep watch at the *Castillo* and, if I saw you leave it, not to follow you out to sea."

"Why on God's earth would any reasonable man think you would?!" Kirkland exploded. "If you were my daughter, I'd take you over my knee and blister your backside!" He took half a step closer. "I've more than half a mind to do it now anyway!"

Becky sat unflinching and returned his glare.

"'T would do you no good at all," MacKenzie said, calmly extending a hand between them. "Nor the lass either, should the truth be known."

Kirkland paused, then took a step back while still eying her darkly. "It was only a thought. And an almighty great temptation!"

He fell silent for a minute or two and appeared to be thinking.

"All right," he said with a nod of decision. "What's done is done. I can't put you ashore in the wilds of Florida, even if I thought we could spare the time. You'll have to stay on board 'til we can put in at some port."

He paused again to take in a breath. "And by God, you'll earn your keep!" he concluded with a roar. "You'll cook our meals, scrub out the galley, clean our quarters, and swab the decks! Together with every other disagreeable task I can manage to think of!"

Becky simply nodded. "That will be fine," she said calmly. "I never expected to remain on your ship as a passenger."

Kirkland stood there glaring at her for another long moment. "Good!" he growled. Then he turned on his heel and stomped back to the bridge.

10

Since cabin space was severely limited on the schooner, there was little choice but for Becky to share her father's small compartment. Kirkland ordered a pallet and blankets brought into it, along with some men's clothes from the ship's slop chest for her to change into.

These last were too large for her slim build, but they made far more sense in light of her expected duties on board than what she had been wearing. And they were reasonably clean, which was a blessing in the close confines of MacKenzie's cabin. Her soiled and odorous former garments were hung outside on hooks until she could find an opportunity to do some laundry.

Once she'd changed and her father came inside to join her, she gave him a faint smile and held out the large hunting knife she'd brought along when she followed his captors and him out to sea.

He tried to interrogate her about how she'd managed to accomplish this task and get aboard the schooner without being noticed. But she was too tired and seasick right then for long explanations. He only managed to learn that it involved the fact she was a strong swimmer—which he knew—and some stealthy climbing and skulking about while everyone was distracted by getting the ship under way.

Her hands were chafed and raw from some of her exertions, but she said she'd found a bit of grease in the lifeboat that helped them a little. There had also been food and water stowed inside it against emergencies. But she admitted with a grimace that she'd been little tempted by the former.

She fell into an exhausted sleep only minutes after this brief conversation, and except for a few gentle snores, there was not another sound to be heard from her until the following day.

That day dawned fair and sunny, and when she finally made it out on deck to take in breaths of the fresh salt air, she found she was feeling fewer effects of the *mal de mer* than she might have expected. By the time another day and a night had passed, she was relieved to discover that she'd finally begun to get her sea legs.

Kirkland had shown gruff compassion during those two days, giving her only a few light tasks until she grew used to the ship's motion and learned its routine. But afterward he stuck to his earlier promise and put her to work in earnest.

She responded with cheerful goodwill, coiling lines, swabbing decks, cleaning the galley, and scouring the pots and pans—all of it without complaint. She was often helped in these chores by one or more of the sailors when their duties permitted. They seemed to feel protective of her and showed more consideration than their strict, unsmiling captain.

At least in the beginning.

Her most important and appreciated role was that of the ship's cook. She'd learned her way around a kitchen early in life and was well aware of the truth of the old adage "the way to a man's heart is through his stomach." She responded modestly and kept her smiles to herself when her efforts won praise from the crew—and their captain.

This soon led to her taking on the added duties of ship's steward, bringing meals to those who couldn't leave their posts or remained in their quarters for one reason or another. And that brought about the only real unpleasantness she experienced in the course of the voyage. It happened on the very first day she began the task.

She'd been told never to enter the locked cabin of James Tyrone unless another crew member was with her. But all of them were busy just then, and the man's dinner was getting cold. *What could be the harm?* she asked herself. There was no way he could escape from a vessel that was miles away from land.

Tyrone welcomed her with a smile and a courtly bow when she unbolted his door and drew it back. But as she came inside to set the dishes down, he slipped past her and shut the door again, latching it from the inside.

Before she was fully aware of what was happening, his arms had pinned hers to her sides, and his body was pressed up tightly against hers. He turned her around and started forcing her back onto his rough, ill-smelling cot.

James Tyrone knew Becky MacKenzie no better than she knew him. In an instant she'd wrenched herself free and produced a twelve-inch dirk from somewhere inside her baggy men's clothing. Its point made a dimple in the man's unshaven throat as she drew herself up to meet his eyes and spoke with icy contempt.

"You may open that door again now if you please. Or else I will just step over your steaming corpse and open it for myself. I'd really prefer the first, since I've more than enough to do without having to clean up after some bloody fool's stupidity."

Tyrone grimaced and backed toward the entrance. The blade never left its place at his throat.

"Gently now, lass. 'T was only a brief impulse o' the moment. I was so besotted by your beauty that I scarce knew what I was about."

"You knew well enough, I'm thinking. I don't expect it was your first time, though it very nearly was your last."

She quickly shifted the knife to his back as he turned to unlatch the door. When it opened she gave him a push with her free hand and slipped outside, slamming the door in his face.

After that she was content to let a male crewman deliver the prisoner's meals, and he willingly accepted the arrangement. During those times when he was allowed brief stints outside to take in the air, he was more narrowly watched than ever. And she found things to do that kept her busy below or at the farthest end of the ship.

Kirkland ordered a diet of hardtack and water added to Tyrone's confinement. But for the moment at least he decided against any physical punishment. MacKenzie had different ideas when he learned what had happened, but he swallowed his anger and kept his thoughts to himself. He was, after all, just another prisoner here on the *Raven*.

And in truth he couldn't help feeling just a touch of fatherly pride at the way Rebecca had handled herself.

His feelings were more mixed as he continued to watch the budding friendship between his daughter and the American officer. Kirkland's anger and consternation at her stowing away had seemed remarkably short lived. Now it looked like there was scarcely a moment, when their respective duties permitted, that the two of them weren't together.

And MacKenzie could only wonder darkly what it was they found to talk about on all those occasions.

11

On the fourth day after they left St. Augustine, Jeremiah and John Robert MacKenzie finally made it back to the homestead. The news that their father and sister had not yet returned was surprising and a little disturbing, but it still seemed too early to worry very much about them.

It was a long way from the ancient city, and the two missing family members were both capable and knowledgeable travelers in the wilderness. Most likely they'd met some kind of unexpected delay, and all would be explained in good time.

Mary was still not entirely used to life on the frontier, and she'd had more time to fret in everybody's absence. She came out onto the veranda to greet her husband and brother-in-law as soon as they'd turned their horses over to Carlos and climbed up the steps.

"I've been so worried," she said, hugging John Robert tightly. "No sign of anyone, and no word."

"Well, we're here now, honey. An' I reckon we'll see the old bull and that wild heifer of our sister in no more'n another day or so. We'll get the story from 'em then. Prob'ly just got so wrapped up in that city life they plum forgot about comin' home."

But "another day or so" came and went with no appearance of Becky and MacKenzie. Mary grew more and more concerned. She'd become very fond of her father-in-law and the girl she thought of as her younger sister.

She said little to John Robert about it, but he knew and understood how she felt. And frankly, he was starting to get worried himself. This was still a sparsely settled country, and any sort of thing might happen. There were roving bands of outlaws and renegades, any of whom might be tempted by the gold their father carried. Or by their horses and outfits. There were dangerous animals, too: bears and panthers, alligators and venomous snakes.

Finally there came a morning when Jeremiah and John Robert's eyes met across the breakfast table.

"You reckon it's time?" Jeremiah asked.

John Robert nodded. "Past time, could be. Though I don't like to think about it."

Mary got up from the table without a word and went to tell Maria to pack food for a journey. The brothers started gathering their weapons and gear; then they asked Carlos to saddle the horses and bring them around front.

It was well before noon when the entire household gathered before the house to see the two off. John Robert hugged Mary and whispered in her ear, "We'll find 'em. No matter where they are an' however long it takes. Might be away for a spell."

"I know." Mary nodded.

"You reckon you'll be all right here all by your lonesome?"

"I reckon." She smiled. She was already starting to pick up some of the language of the frontier. "And I won't be alone. Carlos and Maria will be with me. Between us I think we'll manage just fine."

"All right." John Robert knew there'd be little to do around the ranch at this season. The cattle could fend for themselves, and it was too early for most crops to be put in. He kissed her and gave her arm a squeeze.

Then he turned away and mounted, joining Jeremiah, who was already in the saddle. They left the homestead at a shambling trot.

Their plan was to search along the trail Becky and their father would likely follow coming back from St. Augustine. If this turned up nothing, they'd continue on to the old city and ask around until they found some answers.

They'd no suspicion at that moment where their search would finally lead them.

Several days later in St. Augustine, the brothers had learned almost nothing that was useful. Governor White, who was friendly with their father, had been away during his visit. One of his assistants seemed to recall a brief encounter with a young lady, who might or might not have been their sister. But except that she'd asked to see the governor, he couldn't tell them anything more.

After checking at the various livery stables, they discovered the two horses quartered there. The hostler remembered the young woman who'd brought them—and the gold coin she'd given him for their upkeep. But aside from the suggestion of more of those in the future, she'd said nothing to him about herself or any other plans.

They gave him another coin from the small supply they'd brought with them, with a request that he ask around and let them know whether he learned anything or if she happened to return. So far there'd been no word from him.

Although both the brothers spoke Spanish, they found the townsfolk tended to be tight-lipped and suspicious of strangers. Apart from the colony of Minorcans, who kept their affairs private even from the Spaniards, most of the residents were soldiers, government officials, or their families.

Then, as luck would have it, a storm one day kept the fishing fleet in the harbor. At a grog shop near the waterfront, always a likely enough place for seeking information, they came across a man who'd spent the entire afternoon there with sufficient potables in his system to encourage him to talk freely.

As it turned out, he'd originally been from England, and he seemed to take a special delight in recounting the curious doings of all these "foreigners."

"Big red-headed bloke, was 'e? 'Companied by a li'l slip uv a thing wiv sommat the like colorin'?"

Jeremiah and John Robert looked at one another and then took seats at the table across from the man. "That sounds like them," John Robert said.

"I heard the story after. Wa'n't rightly there on the spot, y' see."

"Uh-huh. So what was it you heard?"

"Well, 't seems they was accosted by some o' them green-coated sojer-boys, just yonder on the quay outside there. They was a few words spoke, an' then the sojers marched that big feller right off to the *Castillo*. Like a prisoner, he was."

"And the girl?" Jeremiah leaned forward. "What happened to the girl?"

"No one 'pears to know. 'Least not any o' them as talked to me about it. Ha'n't heard any word uv her since, neither."

John Robert frowned. "Well, I reckon that's more than we've found out so far. But it ain't a whole lot, is it?"

"Wait," the fisherman said, downing the last of his ale and wiping his mouth with his forearm. When he lowered the tankard, he held it at an angle so they could tell it was empty. "There's sommat more to the story you boys might want to hear."

Jeremiah nodded and got up to get the man a refill. John Robert waited in silence.

After the fisherman had taken a long pull from his newly full tankard, he set it down and leaned forward conspiratorially. "'T seems on the very next day followin' what I was describin', some o' them sojers went to look in on the prisoner an' he wa'n't nowhere to be found. Nor the others they say was locked up in there with 'im. 'Peared they all managed to fly the coop some way in the dark o' the night."

John Robert shook his head. "We've been askin' questions 'round here for a couple days. Why you reckon this is the first time we've heard 'bout it?"

The fisherman held up his hand and rubbed a finger and thumb together. "Word is there was a mite o' gold to change hands. It's common enough wi' these papist heathens."

"Bribery!" Jeremiah said softly. "That could explain a lot of things."

John Robert nodded. "So where do you think the prisoners might have got to?"

"Ha'n't heard nothin' 'bout that." The fisherman shrugged. "But then there was another curious thing happened around the same time."

"What was it?"

"Vessel that was brought into the harbor a couple days ago, fine-lookin' schooner was said to be caught transportin' slaves. She up an' disappeared too. One evenin' she was lyin' at anchor calm as could be, an' by mornin's first light she wa'n't anywhere to be seen."

The brothers asked a few more questions, but it was clear the fisherman had nothing more to offer. They thanked him and gave him money for another ale. Then they left the place and went outside.

The storm had spent itself by now, and the evening sky was clearing. But water still dripped from the trees and eaves while the stones under their feet glistened from the runoff. The air was heavy with moisture and filled with the scent of the sea.

The brothers had learned more than enough this evening to give them food for thought. They walked along the quay until the came to a secluded place where they could talk things over in private.

"You reckon Pa went away on that boat?" Jeremiah asked.

"I got a notion he might of. But if he did, I don't reckon it was of his own choosin'. Not with Becky still somewheres about. Whoever paid to get him out of that jail had a reason to do it. An' maybe for takin' the schooner too. Now what we got to do is find somebody could tell us a deal more."

"Could be time," Jeremiah said with a scowl, "we went to askin' our questions a tad more forcefully."

"Might be," John Robert agreed. "Save us some time."

They continued on down the quay, headed in the direction of the Spanish *Castillo.*

"You got any notion who it is could be behind this?" Jeremiah asked after a minute.

"Maybe," John Robert said quietly. But he didn't explain.

12

The MacKenzie brothers took up a position a hundred yards from the fortress, not too far from the old city gate. There they waited in the shadows for the garrison's watch to change. Most of the soldiers lived someplace else, often with their wives and other family members.

They'd decided they'd remain there all night if need be. But it didn't take that long. A bell within the coquina walls struck the hour, and soon from up St. George Street came the sound of marching feet.

As the brothers slipped back into a narrow alley between buildings, the shadows of a torchlit procession appeared. Before long a dozen Spanish soldiers came into sight, headed by an officer.

Jeremiah put his mouth next to John Robert's ear. "Flew the coop in the middle of the night, the man said."

"Uh-huh."

"Likely some of those are who got paid to let 'em go."

"Uh-huh."

The file of soldiers was straggling a bit, while the officer kept his eyes fixed on their destination. It was almost too easy for the scions of MacKenzie.

They waited in darkness until the column was almost past. Then the last man in line was seized by three strong hands with another clamped over his mouth. He was dragged struggling into the alley and thrown on the ground. Jeremiah sat on him with the sharp edge of his knife—a twin of MacKenzie's—pressed against his throat.

The man ceased to struggle, and his eyes grew wide with fear as he looked up into the grimly smiling face of the younger brother. All fight had now gone out of him. He lay still and silent while the sounds of marching feet grew fainter and then faded away as the column entered the grassy embankment in front of the *Castillo*.

"Reckon they're goin' to miss this feller?" Jeremiah said softly to his brother.

"Prob'ly sooner than later," John Robert replied. "So we need to make this fast."

Jeremiah nodded, and the tip of his knife gently pricked at the soldier's throat. "Listen up, fella. You can die slow or you can die fast. 'T all depends on how much you tell us 'bout those prisoners you-all let out t' other night.

"*N . . . no comprendo!*"

Jeremiah repeated the threat in Spanish, twitching the knife slightly.

"*No . . . no nada sabeo!*"

"You don't, huh?" He shifted the point of the knife to where the man could see it hovering a fraction of an inch beside his left eye. "Well, you just *sabe* this. We ain't in no mood to waste around here. So *dice verdad!*"

The Spaniard gulped, swallowed hard, and then started to talk. He'd suddenly lost all desire to keep secrets from this Anglo who was now threatening to blind him.

He described the two *Norteamericanos* with gold coins to give away for nothing more than taking an hour or two away from their posts. What they'd in mind to do they hadn't said, and no one had asked. It was a bit of an embarrassment the next day when the prisoners were found missing. But their officer didn't seem surprised or upset about it. He'd probably gotten some coins for himself.

"What about that schooner in the harbor—*la goleta*—that went missin'?" John Robert leaned closer. "You know anything about that?"

The knife had been pulled back slightly, and the soldier bobbed his head. "Miguel, *mi compadre*, he told me he got a coin of gold too. For letting the *Americanos* seize the ship. They sailed at night with the tide."

"Any notion of where they were headed?"

The man gave a slight shrug. "*No es seguro*. But Miguel, he thinks maybe he hears the word Apalachicola."

"Apalachicola?" Jeremiah looked at his brother. "Ain't that the river away off yonder in West Florida?"

"Uh-huh. Right about where that Kirkland feller was thinkin' to meet up with some Injuns."

They turned the soldier loose with another gold coin and orders to make himself scarce until morning. They needed the time to plan and prepare before their actions were reported to the garrison.

"You weren't really goin' to put that man's eye out, were you?" John Robert asked as they strode swiftly away.

Jeremiah shrugged. "Well, prob'ly not. But wasn't any call to make my mind up as things turned out."

John Robert and Jeremiah had no ship and no possible way they could think of to get one—even if they were knowledgeable enough to sail it when they did. What they did have was horses: their own and the two their father and sister had ridden to St. Augustine. And since they now realized they had some catching up to do, the spare mounts would be a big help in that department.

They planned to travel overland to the Apalachicola River following the old Spanish mission trail. Since they knew the length of the Florida peninsula as well as their father, the delay in finding out what they had just discovered about the schooner's probable destination and then getting under way was not the great disadvantage it might at first appear. By land it was more than two hundred miles to the river. By sea it was easily ten times that far.

Of course, a vessel at sea wouldn't need to stop and camp for the night. But still they thought they wouldn't be so very far behind when they finally made it to the river.

What they'd do when they got there was something they could not plan, and they wasted no time on idle speculation. Perhaps they'd be able to locate signs of the schooner or its occupants somewhere along the banks. Or they might seek information from friendly Indians. They might even find an English trader they could question.

The important thing for now was to place themselves in the same general area as their kidnapped father. They'd make plans from there.

As for Becky, they'd reluctantly decided they'd just have to leave her to her own devices for the present. They made another fast canvass of the city on the morning they left and still could find no one who remembered seeing her in the days following her visit to the stable. Leaving her here without her palomino pony was a difficult choice. But the brothers decided their need for it was greater under the circumstances.

She was smart and self-reliant and presumably had a gold coin or two left. She should have little trouble finding a way back to the homestead when she wished.

If she wished. John Robert had been wondering about that and had been struck with a crazy notion. It was so crazy, in fact, that he'd decided not to mention it even to his brother.

For their part they'd be traveling relatively light under the circumstances. They had their blanket rolls and slickers, long Kentucky rifles with powder and ball, and two large hunting knives. What remained of the food they'd brought from home was supplemented by a few small purchases from the Spaniards, the most important of which were coffee and salt—two things no man on the frontier would willingly do without. They also bought a small lightweight cooking pot for coffee and stews.

The meat they'd provide for themselves. Both men were skilled hunters, and wild Florida never lacked for game.

By early afternoon they'd left the city and the nearby San Sebastian River behind. They took a Spanish ferry from Picolata across the broad St. Johns and by night were well into the East Florida wilderness. They had hopes of reaching the banks of the Apalachicola in something less than a week.

13

After an otherwise uneventful southerly cruise, the *Raven* swung her bow west to enter the Florida Straits.

If he'd any doubts before, MacKenzie saw clearly during that hazardous passage that Kirkland and his crew were highly capable seamen. With frequent soundings and a watchful lookout above, they threaded their way among hidden reefs and countless small islets to make it beyond the westernmost keys in only a few days.

Once they were well out of sight of any small fishing settlements in the area, they turned north and began the long crossing of the Gulf of Mexico toward the Florida Panhandle.

As the days passed MacKenzie could feel that the air, which had been warm and balmy among the keys, was steadily growing colder. It was no great surprise, for he well knew the length of the southern peninsula. Yet, even so, it felt like an untimely change of seasons. And he found he spent less time on the open deck.

At long last there was a cry of "Land ho!" from the lookout above, and the *Raven* swung her bow west-southwest to follow the low sandy outline of St. George Island. It would be some thirty or forty miles until its western tip could be rounded and they entered the sheltered confines of Apalachicola Bay. Much of Florida's coast was lined with such barrier islands, offering protection from storms but challenges to navigation as well. There were many shoals and shallows to threaten unwary seamen.

Kirkland explained that he'd also seen an eastern passage around the island on the Spanish and British charts he'd studied. But it was reported to be shallow and gave into a correspondingly shallow St. George Sound. Even with the schooner's light draft, he decided there was no reason to chance it. At best it could mean a long delay in approaching the mouth of the river, and at worst they might find their ship hard aground.

The weather in the open Gulf was fair at present, with a brisk following wind. With luck they would enter Apalachicola Bay sometime tomorrow. From there it was not so very far to the wide entrance of the river.

As MacKenzie stood at the rail gazing off at the slowly passing dunes and the dark green line of forest behind them, Rebecca came and took a place beside him. She said nothing for several moments. Then she asked quietly if he'd join her for coffee in the salon after supper.

He looked over at her, noting the serious expression on her face, and accepted this curiously formal invitation with a faint sense of foreboding.

When he came down the steps and saw Kirkland sitting at the table ahead of him, he'd a suspicion he knew what had brought about those earlier misgivings.

He took a place on the bench across from the young man while his daughter brought coffee out of the galley for all of them. She seated herself opposite MacKenzie and for a long minute simply gazed down at the cup in her hands without speaking. Kirkland, beside her, also said nothing.

At last Becky raised her eyes and met her father's.

"I know you've made it clear, Papa, that you don't want to hear any more talk about the reasons for our mission. But Charles and I have been discussing it."

"Charles," was it? And "our mission"? So now it seemed the two of them were conspiring against him! MacKenzie felt a sudden anger at this brash young American who'd use his daughter to advance his own designs.

But when MacKenzie opened his mouth to berate Kirkland, he looked at Rebecca instead. And closed it again. In spite of her sometimes rash behavior, she'd always shown herself at the core to be an intelligent young woman, one who could and did make her own decisions. Not the sort to be swayed by empty words. At least until now.

If she'd seen the momentary hardening of his eyes, she gave no sign. She simply went on in the same quiet voice as before. "We think there are some more things you ought to consider, or perhaps think about more carefully than you have so far. About what's likely to come with a British capture of Florida. For us. And for the Indians."

She'd a speech prepared, it seemed, one she'd given a fair amount of thought to. The least MacKenzie could do was afford her the courtesy of a hearing. Afterward he *might* reconsider. Or he very well might not.

He took a swallow of coffee and nodded. Then he set the cup down and gave her his full attention.

"As you know," Becky began, "the British have coveted this entire North American continent since the days of John Cabot and Sir Walter Raleigh. Now that the French have sold their interests here and the Spanish have lost a fleet, their hopes are higher than ever. With both Canada and Florida in their hands, they'd be in a fine position to go on and reoccupy the rest of their lost colonies." She paused and glanced at Kirkland.

"Only the infant United States could stand in their way. And it has no army to speak of and not very much of a navy."

The American made a wry face but offered no protest.

"Well, you lived under British rule before," she said, "and I suppose we all can again. Although"—she gave a calculated shrug—"it's said their taxes are high and we could expect a lot of new neighbors—plantations, with their slaves!"

Becky paused to see her father's reaction. His face told her nothing.

"And now with all of that," she pressed on, "what about the Indians?"

MacKenzie raised an eyebrow. "What o' them?"

"As I understand the British plan, they mean to bribe the Creeks and other natives with arms and trade goods, so they'll attack the Spanish and pave the way for their own invasion. If that happens, what will be the outcome?"

MacKenzie shrugged. "They've plenty o' warriors to make killin' raids an' cause a deal o' destruction. But knowin' the Indians, I doubt me there'd be any lastin' effect. After they're done wi' their plunderin' and killin', they'll just go back to their villages for great feasts an' celebrations."

"And then?" Becky looked at him sharply. "If the British take over the Floridas, what will they do about their native allies?"

Her father frowned. He knew the answer but hadn't really thought about it until now. No colonial power would want large numbers of armed natives in their territory—who might later attack them in turn. They'd do whatever they must to disarm, kill, or enslave them. Any survivors would be forced to leave their homeland forever.

"You see?" his daughter said very quietly. "None of this is just about us and our future. It could mean the destruction of an entire people!"

MacKenzie remained frowning in silence for several long minutes. Then he glanced from Rebecca to Kirkland and back again.

"Aye," he said finally. "Y' have made your point, lass. It is indeed a thing that may bear a bit more reflection."

He finished the last of his coffee and stood up. "I will consider it tonight, an' we'll speak of it again on the morrow."

Becky and Kirkland stayed seated quietly at the table while he turned and made his way up onto the deck. Wisely, neither made any move to follow.

When the *Raven* negotiated the western pass into Apalachicola Bay, the sun was still below the eastern horizon. Before another two hours had passed, they were entering the broad mouth of the river of the same name.

Thin tendrils of fog still rose from the dark water as the crew went about reefing the main sails and preparing to continue upstream with jib and topsail alone. There was a brisk breeze from the south, and they made fair progress against the current.

MacKenzie had risen early, as was his habit, although Rebecca had preceded him to start breakfast in the galley. He dressed and went on deck, standing by himself at the rail for long minutes while the fog gradually dissipated and he could finally watch the looming forest of moss-laden trees glide past on either hand.

There had been an icy nip in the air when he first emerged from his cabin. But soon the golden disc of the sun had risen high enough to warm his back and shoulders, and then he was comfortable enough in his buckskin jacket.

He'd thought of many things before retiring the previous night, although less about his decision to help the Americans than any of them might have supposed. His daughter had indeed "made her point," and he had to admit she'd succeeded in her plan to change his earlier way of thinking.

But even more important, he'd been struck by the wisdom and understanding behind her words. Until last evening he'd fondly allowed himself to think of Rebecca merely as a precocious child instead of the fully grown young woman she had clearly become.

It was a realization that made him all the more uncomfortable when he thought of the obvious interest Lieutenant Kirkland had been taking in her. And she in him.

In time the river gradually grew narrower as it wound its way north, although it would remain broad and navigable for many miles. There were occasional sandy shoals or floating trees to impede their progress. But these could be avoided or fended off readily enough by sharp-eyed sailors with pikes and oars.

He spent most of the long day gazing out toward the river's banks while they went slowly past on either side. As always, he found himself remarking on the seemingly endless variety of this Florida country.

At times there were forested bluffs, surmounted by tall pines or thickly clustered hardwoods. At other places his eye could scarcely penetrate the blackness of low, forbidding swamps with bays and strangler vines that stretched out over the shallows.

There was Spanish moss in gray festoons hanging from every limb, except on those rare occasions when the trees suddenly drew back and yielded to some level floodplain carpeted by reeds and sedges.

As the hours passed, Kirkland and Rebecca kept a respectful distance from him, going about their respective duties with no attempt at idle conversation. No doubt they thought it wiser to leave him to himself while he took as much time as he needed to reach a decision.

And Kirkland at least knew they could afford the wait. When the sun dipped below the trees to the west, they were still a number of miles downstream from the place where he hoped to meet with the Indians. He ordered the anchor lowered in mid-river and set a watch for the night.

After supper was over and the dishes cleared away, MacKenzie decided it was finally time to end the suspense. He asked Rebecca and Kirkland to join him for coffee in the salon.

14

He began by questioning the American narrowly about his true intentions in Florida and what he expected to accomplish by making contact with the Indians. He'd heard most of the answers before, but he meant to satisfy himself that there were no hidden motives or plans for a later incursion by their neighbors to the north.

Kirkland answered frankly and with apparent sincerity. There were no telltale signs that he might be keeping something back. Rebecca listened quietly with a frown on her face that revealed impatience with her father's suspicions. But she knew him well enough to simply fold her hands in front of her and keep her thoughts to herself.

At last MacKenzie nodded. "Y'r plans sound straightforward enough, an' as like to benefit the natives as your own nation. I care little for the latter, t' be truthful. But forestallin' any needless loss o' life should at all times be worth the attempt. So I am now prepared to offer what small assistance I can."

Kirkland let out a long, slow breath and grinned. "Splendid! That's what we've all been hoping for from the start!" He covered MacKenzie's hand on the table with his own. "You have earned my deepest gratitude, as well as that of my nation!"

"Do not be so generous wi' y'r thanks just yet," the older man said seriously. "What I offer may be a good deal less than y' hope or expect." He sat back on the bench and folded his arms. "I'll gladly serve to translate from one language to another an' may lend y' some knowledge o' the natives' thinkin' an' their customs. But as for havin' a say in what each o' them will do once we've seen 'em, that is beyond the power o' any outsider, be he white man or red. Everyone will choose his path for himself."

MacKenzie saw Kirkland's curious frown and went on.

"Y' see, the native is an individual foremost an' last. They have their chiefs, selected for wise counsel an' experience. But none o' those can command a single action by a single member o' their tribe." He smiled wryly at the American. "Unlike y'r own much-vaunted 'democracy'!"

Kirkland nodded slowly. "I see. So our hopes must lie in persuasion, not of a few but of the many. That's a daunting prospect."

"It is. But t' will be the only chance that we have."

After a minute of thoughtful silence, Kirkland went on to ask in more detail about what he might expect in a meeting with the Indians—should it be possible to arrange one. He was also hoping for suggestions about how they might first make contact with them and request a general gathering where they might present their case to the tribe.

But for the last MacKenzie had little advice to offer at this stage. Everything would depend on whom they happened to meet initially and the attitude of those toward the unfamiliar white visitors.

He did advise that if they were able to be invited to an Indian gathering, they should take along as many men as possible, leaving only a few behind to keep watch over the *Raven*. It was always best to negotiate from a position of strength to the greatest extent possible.

And for the same reason, all who went should go armed. Carrying weapons on the frontier was a matter of custom as well as prudence. The natives would of course have their own weapons, and coming into their country empty-handed could be viewed as a dangerous sign of weakness.

After a time there seemed nothing more to be discussed for the present. Becky wished them both good night and left the salon. The men stayed behind over a final cup of coffee.

MacKenzie felt a momentary urge to question Kirkland about his intentions toward his daughter. But he immediately thought better of it and said nothing.

The silence that followed seemed companionable enough. But perhaps it wasn't quite so comfortable as it might have been.

Late in the afternoon of the following day they dropped anchor in a small cove overlooked by high limestone bluffs on the eastern side of the river. The area above these was heavily forested, giving no indication of what might lie beyond. There were ragged jumbles of driftwood here and there, left over from previous floods. Some of these were many feet above the water.

The western bank, though not as steep, was thickly forested as well. And in at least one place the dense tangled growth of a swamp could be seen.

On both sides the winter foliage was a colorful blend of red, green, and gold. A number of the hardwoods had lost their leaves, but many had kept their fall colors to mingle with the darker hues of cedars and other evergreens.

They were now well inside the territory ruled by the Creek Nation, and Kirkland was anxious to make contact with them as soon as possible in hopes of setting up a meeting with some of their leaders and members of the tribe.

As it happened, this occurred sooner and presented less of a challenge than either he or MacKenzie had expected. Word of their coming had been passed forward by native watchers along the shore well in advance of their arrival at this place. Almost the moment their anchor struck the water, a band of warriors emerged from the trees on the rock-strewn eastern bank, demanding to know who they were and what their business was here in Creek lands.

MacKenzie responded in their language, assuring them that he and his companions were friendly and simply hoped for a meeting with members of the tribe. After a lengthy discussion that Kirkland couldn't follow, a few of the men from the schooner were allowed to come ashore—bringing customary gifts as advised by MacKenzie.

They followed the warriors up through the rocks and into a small clearing surrounded by trees. There the gifts were presented and accepted with due ceremony, after which all of them sat down in a circle and the talking began.

Well, nearly everyone was sitting. A couple of the warriors stood back among the trees to one side, looking curiously out toward the river where the *Raven* lay at anchor.

Kirkland understood little of what was said. MacKenzie took the lead and only occasionally spared the time to translate. Yet, whenever he did, he made sure he showed deference to his "chief" so that none of the Indians would be in doubt as to who the visitors' leader was.

It all seemed to take an uncommonly long time, and MacKenzie once told him briefly that "getting straight to the point" was not the natives' way. They wanted to observe and assess the speakers, as well as hear what they had to say.

After an hour or so, the Indians seemed to grow less wary, listening carefully and nodding occasionally when MacKenzie spoke.

At last it was decided that a council might be arranged at a nearby village within the next day or two. As it happened, two of the most influential chiefs in this part of the Creek Nation were currently staying there. Messengers would be sent ahead while the rest of the warriors camped at this place for the night. Tomorrow they'd conduct Kirkland and his party to the village.

When the meeting finally ended, once again with due ceremony, everyone returned to the riverbank and Kirkland's group boarded their skiff to return to the schooner. As the two sailors who'd been with them bent to their oars, Kirkland turned to MacKenzie with a smile of satisfaction.

"That all worked out much better than I expected," he said. "Thanks to you."

"Aye, 't went well enough." MacKenzie nodded. "But I wonder, did y' happen to notice those two lookin' off at our vessel while we talked?"

"Yes. I suppose they'd never seen such a large ship before."

"Perhaps. But more important, they were countin'. Now they've a good sense o' our numbers, an' they know they've little to fear from the few we've got wi' us." He paused and glanced back to where the Indians could be seen moving about through the trees making camp.

"Was it m'self," he said, turning to meet Kirkland's eyes, "I'd set a double watch for this night an' keep weapons to hand." He shrugged. "The native's as honorable as any man, I reckon. But 't is not the part o' good sense to put temptation in his way."

When they'd climbed aboard the schooner, MacKenzie saw that Tyrone was taking his "evening constitutional" near the bow. A sailor stood with him, but that man's attention was fixed on the shore, watching the Indians with curious fascination.

He was about to speak to Kirkland about the man's lack of caution when the sailor suddenly yelped and bent forward clutching his midsection. Tyrone shoved him roughly aside and swiftly vaulted the rail. There was a loud splash from the far side of the ship.

MacKenzie leapt forward. But before he could reach the spot where Tyrone had stood, there was another splash from the same direction. He gripped the rail and leaned far over, scanning the turbulent waters below.

He could make out two men in the fading light, grappling and cursing and striving to trade blows within a boiling welter of man-made cataracts. MacKenzie threw off his coat and straddled the rail. But then he saw a dripping fist rise up above the vortex and come down with a bone-jarring thwack!

An instant later, there was a shout from below: "I have him now, m' lads! He's no longer feelin' quite so warlike as once he did!" There was a pause. Then, "Still, 't is a tiresome burden supportin' him here. A friendly hand to hoist him aboard would scarce be amiss!"

Before MacKenzie could enter the water, two of the sailors had jumped in. He stepped back to recover his coat and watched while a groggy Tyrone was manhandled aboard, followed by a soaked and grinning Michael O'Shaughnessy.

"Sure, it's a grand Irish spirit that one has! But there's more than one can play at the game. An' it may be that some did spend a few nights more i' the back streets o' the world!"

"Throw him in his cabin and lock the door!" A glowering Charles Kirkland stood over them with his fists on his hips. "No supper for him tonight!" He whirled on the sailor Tyrone had knocked aside. "Nor for you either! I'd clap you in irons if we weren't so short-handed. If I ever catch you woolgathering again, I won't be so lenient!"

When the prisoner had been secured and blankets brought for the shivering men who'd been in the water, Kirkland turned to O'Shaughnessy and held out a hand. "I owe you a debt of thanks, sir. You could just as easily have taken the chance to abandon us yourself."

O'Shaughnessy pulled the blanket more tightly around him and accepted the hand. "Sure an' I could," he said. "But to what purpose, i' truth? I've no wish to spend long days skulkin' through the wilds wi' murderin' savages at every hand. The victuals here are good, wi' a drop o' the craythur now an' again." He shrugged. "An' where might I be goin' to besides? I've no kith nor kin anywhere nearby."

"Y' might o' gone to the British," MacKenzie said, "as I've small doubt Tyrone had in his mind. 'T is likely they'd pay well for news o' our presence."

"The British, is it?" O'Shaughnessy gave him a dark look and made as if to spit on the deck before he thought better of it. "Shame be upon you for a fallen scion o' the Celtic race! I'd sooner roast in Gehenna than share a wink or a nod wi' aught o' their kind!"

"Well, whatever your reasons, we're grateful," Kirkland said. "And if there's something I can do to show it, you've only to ask."

"I've been well content here," O'Shaughnessy began. Then he paused and seemed to consider. "But now as you're makin' me the offer"—he looked over toward Indian encampment beside the river—"there might be a small favor you could do me, were you so inclined." After another moment, he went on.

"I've no great love for the savages, whom I met in mortal combat these many years since. An' still I've a touch o' the curiosity even so. I have never been to a village to see how they live. Do y' suppose, should you now travel to one for a meetin', I might come as one o' the party?"

Kirkland studied him thoughtfully for a long moment. Then he glanced at MacKenzie, remembering his earlier advice to take as large a group as possible to any such meeting. He shrugged. "I can't think of a good reason why not just at the moment. But let's go below and talk more about it."

MacKenzie let the others precede him down the steps, hanging back briefly with a thoughtful frown on his face. It could be his imagination. But it seemed to him now that the "drunken Irishman" he'd grown so used to disparaging was as sober as himself!

15

The morning sun was still well below the eastern bluffs when those aboard the *Raven* finished their breakfasts and made their way up on deck. Yet it was clear the Indians had already decamped long since. Now they were seated motionless on the limestone rocks along the shore, gazing silently out toward the schooner and its occupants.

Their placid manner could have given some the impression they were simply idling away the time until those from the ship came to join them. MacKenzie knew better. They were giving thorough attention to everything before them. These strangers in their country were still potential enemies. And their ship might prove a valuable source of arms and provisions. If they displayed no hostile intent just now, it was because all of them knew the value of patience. They would wait and consider carefully before deciding on any action.

Aboard the *Raven* the group that would travel to the village assembled by the rail while the longboat was brought around to take them ashore. These included Kirkland, MacKenzie, Sergeant Jaynes, and a seemingly alert and clear-eyed Michael O'Shaughnessy. Four of the American sailors would come as well, leaving the other two behind to guard the ship and keep an eye on Tyrone.

Becky would remain on board as well, despite her bitter protests.

"I speak Muskogee at least as well as you," she told her father, putting her fists on her hips and thrusting out her chin. "Wouldn't two translators be better than one? As well as another armed companion?"

"I doubt me they'd allow a woman to speak in council," MacKenzie said mildly, "on the first account. An' as for the second"—he rested a gentle hand on her shoulder—"I'd simply feel easier in the mind were y' not to be placin' y'rself at risk when there's no' the need."

He raised no questions about her knowledge of the native tongue or her competence with weapons. He was aware of both, though he'd private doubts that either was quite so great as she herself believed.

Every man who was to make the journey had armed himself from the schooner's ample weapons locker. MacKenzie carried a long rifle he'd found there and the broad sheathed knife his daughter had returned to him. O'Shaughnessy had slung a baldric with a Spanish rapier over his shoulder. The others took with them a variety of pistols, cutlasses, and dirks.

They also wore light canvas packs containing food for themselves and more gifts for their hosts, intending to make a further show of goodwill.

As MacKenzie had predicted, none of the Indians showed the least surprise or concern about the weapons the newcomers had with them. Each of those carried his own personal assortment of war clubs, hatchets, spears, and bows. Nor were they unaware that they presently outnumbered their visitors by a factor of more than two to one.

A low mist lay over the river as the white men left the longboat and came ashore. MacKenzie glanced back over his shoulder and had the eerie impression that the *Raven* was floating above the water on a cloud. He could no longer see anything of those who remained on board.

When they'd made their way up the steep bank, everyone assembled in the same clearing where yesterday's meeting had been held. Then the Indians separated into two groups, one of these advancing single file up a narrow trail that topped out on the highest of the eastern bluffs. The others indicated that the visitors should follow, then strung out behind them along the trail.

From the crest of the bluff, they turned north, descending for a little way into a rock-bound depression and then rising again, keeping to the higher ground as much as possible.

The leaders set a steady, tireless pace, up rock-strewn scarps and down into shadowed ravines, then up again across thickly wooded hills that appeared without number. It made MacKenzie think of the mountain country he knew lay many miles to the north. This was a very different Florida from the pine flatlands and boggy sloughs he'd most been accustomed to.

The natives seemed able to maintain their unvarying rate of progress for hours, perhaps even days, without pausing for rest. Not so the less seasoned newcomers. By the time the sun was approaching its zenith and a halt was finally called, MacKenzie and his companions sank gratefully down on the nearest rocks or logs and hardly stirred except to take in deep gulps of the crisp upland air. No one wanted to think about the miles that still might lie ahead.

From his seat on a moss-covered rock, MacKenzie looked about the shaded clearing that was bordered by a swift-flowing stream. He reached up to untie the kerchief from around his neck and mopped his brow. He smiled wryly as he recalled the time many years ago when he'd felt himself as inexhaustible as the Indians. That was when he'd been a youthful long hunter in the Florida wilderness and would have viewed this kind of trek as all in a day's work.

He'd still kept much of his former strength and had allowed himself to believe he'd remained fit enough in later life. But there was no use denying now that the years had taken their toll.

He saw Michael O'Shaughnessy make his way across the clearing toward a large tree at the forest's edge. The Irishman seemed to be holding up at least as well as himself. He was a few years younger, of course. But not all that many, judging from the creases at the corners of his eyes and his graying hair. He'd been uncharacteristically quiet so far during the journey, watching their Indian guides with a wary eye and avoiding any sort of contact with them.

He spied MacKenzie and took a detour to come up and stand beside him. Leaning forward so their heads were almost touching, he spoke in a cautious whisper. "How much farther now do y' think we may trust these godless savages? For aught we know they may at this moment be leadin' us into a bloody ambush."

MacKenzie shrugged and chose not to mention that O'Shaughnessy was present at his own request. "All things are possible," he said quietly, "but I'd think it unlikely. I doubt me they'd be takin' so much trouble about it if that were their plan. Knowin' their numbers an' ours, 't would have been far simpler to put us all to the knife an' seize our vessel in the dark o' the night."

He paused and turned to meet the other man's eyes. "I have learned," he went on, "that the native says little he does not mean. If he says he will take us to his village to meet his chiefs, I'm thinkin' that is precisely what he plans to do." He gave another shrug and then grinned. "At all events we have now crossed the Rubicon, as 't is said. There can be no turnin' back from here."

O'Shaughnessy nodded soberly and said no more. He left MacKenzie to go take a seat on the ground with his back to the broad trunk of a tree. If he was at all reassured by his companion's words, it didn't keep him from watching every slight movement of the Indians in the clearing.

Though they'd brought food from the ship, none of Kirkland's men seemed inclined to eat anything at present. They were simply too exhausted. The Indians ate sparingly of pemmican and roasted corn they carried in their pouches. Then all of them took turns stretching out on their bellies to drink from the stream.

MacKenzie sat watching them with his elbows on his knees. Then he straightened and took the water bottle from his belt to slake his own considerable thirst. As he replaced the cork, he noticed that a young warrior had been observing him curiously from several feet away.

He turned to the youth and said in Muskogee, "How much farther is it to your village now?"

The warrior looked from him to the sky. "There before dark," he said brusquely. Then he strode quickly off to join his comrades as they got ready to resume the journey.

MacKenzie sighed and got wearily to his feet.

It was in fact late afternoon when they came to a broad clearing with a number of log and brush structures arranged about it. Thin feathers of smoke could be seen rising above these into the sky.

As they entered the open space, children and dogs appeared to be everywhere. Women were moving among them, going about their various tasks. All of these stopped whatever they were doing when they spied the travelers' approach. There were welcomes for the returning warriors and wary curiosity directed toward the strangers.

MacKenzie looked around him thoughtfully as they crossed the clearing, noting the many European products that spoke of a flourishing trade between natives and white men. There were cast-iron pots, woolen blankets, steel hatchets, and short-barreled muskets almost every place he looked. Most of these seemed to be of English manufacture, no doubt obtained from the John Forbes Company, which had continued its profitable commerce under Spanish rule.

Their guides conducted them to a large structure in the center of the village, evidently a communal gathering place. They were halted a dozen feet away while one of the warriors stepped forward and pushed apart the blankets that covered the entrance.

He disappeared inside and after several minutes returned followed by two other men, who halted just outside the opening to stand with arms folded while wordlessly appraising the visitors. Their proud and haughty bearing gave little doubt that these were the chiefs Kirkland and his men had journeyed all this distance to meet.

Each was wearing an elaborate combination of European and native dress: thick feathered robes over bright calico tunics, loose cotton breeches, and soft leather boots ornamented with beads and porcupine quills. On their heads were oriental-style turbans surmounted by heron and egret plumes.

The leader of the warriors who had brought MacKenzie and his companions to the village went up to them and spoke respectfully, apparently making some kind of introduction or explanation of their presence.

One of the chiefs, a man with piercing black eyes and a hawk-like nose, responded sharply and made a curt gesture of dismissal. His older companion then raised a hand and spoke calmly and deliberately at more length. Kirkland thought he saw in this man's manner and in his mahogany features, deeply lined by age, something of greater wisdom and patience.

"The younger one's called Nah-ta-lah," MacKenzie told him quietly as they stood next to one another. "An' he wants no part o' us or our doin's."

He listened for another moment. Then, "The older one's not so hasty, it seems. He's tellin' 'em it costs nothin' to hear what we have to say. They can always decide what to do wi' us after."

"A possible ally?" Kirkland asked cautiously. "What is his name?"

"Wa-tah-hoya. But I'd not be makin' any assumptions regardin' him. When we've had our say, he may yet believe we'd all be less trouble to 'em dead."

He felt the young lieutenant stiffen and turned to meet his eyes.

"We're each o' us safe enough here for the present, I think. 'T is not their custom to kill an enemy who comes o' his own will into their village." He shrugged. "As for after, once we're gone from it again . . ." He left the sentence unfinished.

Following a lengthy discussion between the chiefs and others of the warriors, it was finally decided to accept the new arrivals as guests of the village—for this night only. They would dine with their hosts and then be assigned a separate shelter for sleep. Tomorrow they could appear before the assembled village and have a chance to make their case.

They presented the gifts they'd brought for the chiefs, along with what food they had with them. Then, while they waited for the meal to be prepared, MacKenzie recounted to the rest of the party all that had so far been said and decided. He repeated what he'd told Kirkland about his belief that no harm would come to them as long as they remained here in the village.

O'Shaughnessy scowled darkly at this news. But he managed to keep his doubts to himself until after the meal was over and they'd finally retired to their shelter. Then he was one of the first to speak in support of MacKenzie's suggestion that they should take turns sleeping and staying awake during the night in order to keep watch.

Just in case.

16

The next day the entire village assembled to hear the visitors and consider what they had come to say. The air was brisk, but the sky was a clear and brilliant blue, so it had been decided to hold the meeting outdoors in a large amphitheater-like arrangement that was often used for such a purpose. This suited MacKenzie, for he thought it far preferable to the dark and smoky interior of the communal lodge.

The Indians sat on squared-off logs laid out as benches while their chiefs occupied a raised platform at the front and center. The visitors were conducted to a separate row of logs reserved for outsiders a short distance away and facing the assemblage.

All the natives had blankets wrapped around them to ward off the early-morning chill. Kirkland and his party had only the clothes they'd arrived in, but since their outer garments were of wool and leather, these served them well enough for the present. It would not be long before the warming sun rose high enough in the cloudless sky to make them forget any temporary discomfort.

As his eyes roamed across the seated numbers before him, Kirkland was interested to see these included women as well as men. The women appeared to be relegated to a few rows in the rear, but their keen attention was no less for that. He realized during the later discussions that none of them spoke. But he'd a notion that their views would be made clear at a later time.

After a brief ceremony to ask their guiding spirits for wisdom and judgment, the chiefs invited Kirkland, as the leader of the newly arrived delegation, to address the assembly.

He rose, took a moment to gaze across the sea of stoic faces before him, and then started to speak in a firm and confident voice.

Yet his description of the British threat—as translated by MacKenzie—was not met with the sort of concerned response he'd hoped for or expected. In fact, he could see little visible reaction at all. The chiefs and others of the tribe had all listened carefully. But now nothing about their looks or manner gave any clue to their inner thoughts.

Afterward he waited while those in the gathering spent a number of minutes in discussion among themselves. MacKenzie made no effort to translate, only responding to Kirkland's questioning looks by saying, "They're talkin' it over. Most of 'em still favor the Brits, whose traders they all know. They're askin' themselves now just who it is that we are. An' what would be our reason to come here speakin' against 'em."

After what seemed a long time, Wa-tah-hoya held up a hand for quiet and rose gravely to his feet. He met Kirkland's eyes. "You have told us that the English plan to send many soldiers into Florida," he said. "And with these they mean to seize all our lands. We ourselves have heard nothing of this. How is it that you, a stranger, should come to know of it?"

When his question had been translated, Kirkland replied without hesitating.

"Our leaders in the great city of Washington are wise," he said, "as are those of the Creek Nation. We have agents"—MacKenzie used the Muskogee word for "scouts"—"in the land of the English and also among the Spanish. They have learned these things and reported them to us. We've confidence in their knowledge and believe they speak truly."

He paused while his answer was communicated and saw the older man nod his understanding.

Nah-ta-lah stood up abruptly and glared at the visitors with his arms folded across his chest. "You are not of this country," he said haughtily. "We know neither you nor the scouts you claim to have sent. What reason is there for us to believe their words? Or your own, for the matter of that?"

His contempt needed no translation, and Kirkland returned his stare boldly. Yet he waited until MacKenzie had rendered his challenge into English before he responded. "I do not lie," he said coldly. "We have come here into your country with the hope of preventing a war—a war that will cost your people many lives. And your lands too, by the time it is over!"

Nah-ta-lah made a scornful grunt as he heard the translation. "Everything we have seen of your countrymen tells us that they are the ones who want our lands. I think you do lie. You come here only to deceive us and to take what is ours!"

This was followed by an angry murmur among the Indians and much nodding of heads. Kirkland kept his expression neutral while MacKenzie related what the younger chief had said. Then he looked at Wa-tah-hoya and nodded in his turn.

"It is true, there are those among us who've no regard for what others may possess—whether it belongs to the Indian or the white man. I have found this to be so in many places and among many peoples. Yet there are also many wiser men who choose to live in harmony with their brothers!"

While MacKenzie translated this, Kirkland shifted his attention from the chiefs to the faces of their followers. He saw little to suggest his last words had made a favorable impression. But neither was there much in their expressions to suggest that they hadn't.

After a long minute, he spread his hands apart. "No one can tell you what the future may bring. Today I speak only of the present. And I believe at present there is great danger for you and your people." He paused. "You have heard my words. The course you take is for you to decide."

Then he sat down.

MacKenzie completed the translation and resumed his own seat. He realized he'd been much impressed by the young lieutenant's poise and self-command. He'd an idea the Indians had been as well. But what they would choose to do was an entirely different question. And as he'd more than half expected, there would be no immediate answer.

"We thank you for your words," Wa-tah-hoya said gravely. "We will consider them with care." He raised his hand in a gesture of dismissal. "You may return to your vessel now. We grant you safe passage until you have reached it."

Nah-ta-lah made an angry sound, but the older man didn't seem to hear him. "Beyond that," he concluded, "there will be no assurances."

MacKenzie translated, and Kirkland nodded. He rose and thanked the chiefs and the tribe for their attention. Then he then turned away and led his followers out of the village.

17

There were no native guides for the return trip. But from long habit, MacKenzie had paid careful attention to their surroundings and their back trail all during the earlier journey. As soon as the village was well behind them, he took the lead without hesitation.

They walked in silence for a time. Then, when the trail widened out enough to permit it, Kirkland moved up beside him. "What do you think?" he asked. "Did we accomplish anything back there?"

MacKenzie shrugged. "I canna' be sure. No more than y'rself. Old Wa-tah-hoya would much prefer to bide his time, I think, an' wait upon developments. But Nah-ta-lah an' the younger braves are spoilin' for a fight. It is their usual way o' gainin' wives, prestige, an' property." He paused and glanced over at his companion. "Speakin' o' the last, did y' happen to see all the English goods the natives had among 'em?"

"I did. A sly piece of bribery from those London-based traders, do you think?"

"Aye, 't is likely. At all cases, it is a resource the Indians would no' wish to be without."

They walked on together in silence for several more minutes. MacKenzie seemed to be thinking.

"Y' know," he said then, "there is about this affair a thing might offer us a wee shred o' hope."

"What's that?"

"There has been no mention o' the Seminoles thus far. Y' had no word o' them from any o' y'r higher-ups in Washington?"

"No. Who are they?"

"They have become a separate people now, though 't is not so well known outside the Floridas. An' they've scant love for the others o' their Creek brethren. If the British are countin' their numbers into their plans for a native risin', they may well be disappointed. It could even be they'd face resistance from a different quarter."

Kirkland shrugged and said nothing. It was a thing to be considered, though any advantage it offered seemed small and remote under the circumstances.

The trip back to the schooner was long but uneventful. There was no sign of any Indians along the way, though MacKenzie had little doubt that some would be following along and watching. They'd want to keep a wary eye on their recent guests until they could be sure they'd left the country.

The sun had dipped below the western treetops, and the sky was streaked with red and gold when they climbed the final bluff to look down through the branches on the lagoon where the *Raven* waited. She appeared much the same as when they'd left her, her sails well reefed and her anchor line taut from the river's current. The dark waters moved slowly past, highlighted by a few silver ripples here and there as the last remnants of daylight found their way among the trees.

The view in its entirety was one of serene and timeless beauty. MacKenzie thought it a subject some skillful landscape artist might have chosen for a painting.

There was only one slightly discordant note that he didn't become fully aware of until he'd spent some several minutes atop the height recovering his breath. When it occurred to him to mention it to Kirkland, he found that the younger man had already begun his descent to the water's edge.

As soon as he'd emerged from the trees onto the rocks below, the lieutenant called out loudly to the crewmen he'd left on the ship. He received no reply and continued to make his way farther down the steep bank before repeating his hail. Again there was no response.

By the time MacKenzie had managed to reach the place where Kirkland now stood with most of his men, the silence from the schooner had stretched into several long minutes. Nor had anyone appeared on deck.

"Something's wrong," Kirkland said sharply. "No one aboard there seems to be on watch."

"Aye." MacKenzie gave Jaynes his rifle and started stripping off his coat and removing his boots. "I saw as much from yon height above." As he entered the water, there was a faint, muffled cry from somewhere inside the ship.

He struck out for the vessel with powerful strokes and was followed moments later by two of the sailors who'd been in their party.

They scrambled up the rope ladder, which for some unknown reason had been left over the side. As soon as he'd made it past the rail, MacKenzie called out. He received a response that seemed to come from the forward cabin occupied by James Tyrone. The voice was weaker now, scarcely more than an agonized groan.

They hurried to the place and found the door closed and padlocked. No one had with him any keys, so one of the sailors went to seize a marlinspike from a nearby locker. Between them they quickly managed to rip the hasp from the bulkhead.

In the fading daylight from the open door, they saw two prone figures on the deck inside. Spreading out around each of them was a dark pool of what appeared to be blood.

They rushed in and knelt beside the figures, quickly discovering that one of the two was dead. He'd been pierced through the neck by some kind of a blade. The other's head was a tangled mass of hair and gore, but his eyes fluttered open when MacKenzie's hand touched his shoulder.

"Gulled!" he croaked, his voice barely more than a whisper. "Gulled by that grinnin' shanty Irishman!" He tried to raise himself up, but the effort brought forth a groan of agony. He lay back and closed his eyes.

"The girl!" MacKenzie gripped his shoulder roughly, trying to keep him from fainting. "Rebecca!" he almost shouted. "What's happened to my girl?"

The injured man's eyes slowly reopened, and he gazed bleakly up at the man kneeling by him. "Gone!" he rasped after a moment.

"Gone!" MacKenzie bent closer. "Gone where?"

"Taken . . . by Tyrone." Then the sailor's eyes rolled up, and he lost his battle for consciousness.

MacKenzie sat back on his heels and slowly lowered his chin to his chest. He remained without moving for several long minutes. Finally he looked up at the sailor who was lighting a lantern overhead.

"He still breathes," he said quietly. "Do what y' can for him."

He rose to his feet and found the second sailor watching from the entrance. "An' you, lower a boat an' fetch those others waitin' on the shore."

The man nodded and quickly left to go about this task.

MacKenzie followed him onto the deck and crossed to the far rail. He gripped it with fingers that turned white at the knuckles and stood for a long time, staring out over the water toward the dark trees that loomed in the west.

When he finally spoke, there was no one there to hear. "There's plans to be made," he said very quietly, "an' a pursuit to be about!"

18

Kirkland and his men responded to Tyrone's actions with a rage that almost equaled MacKenzie's own. Curses, bitter words, and violent threats filled the air the instant Becky's kidnapping was reported. But words are not deeds, and the matter of what to do about it remained to be determined.

The injured sailor was moved to a comfortable berth with a man assigned to watch over him. Another sailor was posted on watch. MacKenzie and the two who'd been in the water with him took off their clothes to dry them by a freshly built fire in the small galley. Then, wrapped in blankets, they joined the rest in the *Raven's* salon to discuss the situation and decide what to do next.

Their number was small: only six out of the eight able-bodied men who were still on board. MacKenzie, Kirkland, Jaynes, and O'Shaughnessy sat at the table, while the two sailors stood by the entrance. All of them had mugs of freshly brewed coffee in their hands.

The mood of the moment brought forth a furious spate of talk from five of these calling for pursuit and immediate vengeance. Various schemes were loudly put forward and as loudly rejected.

But the reality of the situation soon intervened. The schooner's safety was of first importance, for the Indians had given no promise they wouldn't attack after the crew had returned to it. Their reduced numbers only made the risk greater. If there was to be a pursuit, who would take part and who would stay behind?

MacKenzie kept silent while the angry talk ran its course. He understood the men's urgent desire to do *something* instead of just sitting idly by. But he'd long ago made his decision. He'd go after Tyrone and his daughter alone.

It had been many years since he'd used his skills as a tracker in the Florida wilderness. But those skills weren't forgotten. He'd have himself put ashore at first light tomorrow and search out the trail of the two from the ship. He'd no doubt that he would find it or that he could follow wherever it led.

Sooner or later he was sure to catch up with them. And when he did, he meant to settle that old unfinished business with the former pirate once and for all. The very last thing he needed on such a quest was a gaggle of angry tender-feet thrashing through the woods in his wake!

After what seemed a long and pointless discussion, Lieutenant Kirkland held up his hand for silence. He looked slowly around at each person in the room.

"There is no one here," he said with rigidly contained emotion, "who wants to go after Beck—Rebecca—any more than I do. And to save her from the clutches of that scoundrel Tyrone!" He paused and took a deep breath.

"But I am very much afraid I can't permit myself that luxury right now. I . . . we . . . came here to Florida with a mission: one that sets the future of two nations, our own and the Creeks', in the balance against that of one very . . . admirable . . . young woman. With the Indians' intended actions still uncertain and the threat of a British invasion now close upon us, we must sail for Pensacola without delay. The Spaniards must be warned of the danger in time to seek re-inforcements from Mexico or Cuba." He paused again.

"I'll need my entire crew to do that," he concluded grimly, "including Sergeant Jaynes. We're even more short-handed now than we were at the start!" He glanced across the table. "Mister MacKenzie's help would be welcome as well. But I'd not be so heedless as to ask a father to abandon his daughter."

An' well that you wouldn't, MacKenzie thought to himself. *For there's no quantity o' askin' could avail y' a whit.*

Kirkland placed both hands on the table and stood up. "We weigh anchor tomorrow at dawn. Everyone have a bite of cold supper; then get whatever rest that you can."

There was silence as he left the salon to go up on deck. No one voiced any objection to the commander's decision, either while he was speaking or afterward. Jaynes and the sailors were used to following orders. But it seemed they had also realized, in the face of cold reality, that there was no other real choice. Even O'Shaughnessy had simply nodded his head quietly.

As for MacKenzie, it was only what he'd planned on from the first.

He retired to his cabin and stretched out on the bunk. For a long time he lay in the darkness, unable to sleep while a procession of dire thoughts vied for his attention. Then, with an effort, he pushed these aside and decided to use the hours of enforced wakefulness to give more thought to the task that lay ahead.

First, he asked himself, where would Tyrone most likely be going? To the British, he felt almost certain. As he'd told O'Shaughnessy, they could be expected to pay well for information about Kirkland's activities in Florida. And only one small warship of the most powerful navy on earth would be needed to send the *Raven* and her handful of men to the bottom of the Gulf.

So where might the closest Englishmen be found? The headquarters of the John Forbes Company was in Pensacola, and Kirkland had said that an agent of the British government might be among its employees. At the Spanish port Tyrone might also board a ship to take him to some distant part of the world.

There were other possibilities, but these seemed highly unlikely. English traders conducted their business all over East and West Florida, from the Georgia border to the upper St. Johns. But those places seemed impossibly distant through miles of untamed wilderness, or else they were situated near Indian villages. MacKenzie and his companions had good reason to know that these last would be wary of European strangers in their lands. It was a risk Tyrone would not be anxious to take.

So Pensacola must be his destination. It would still be a long trek through miles of wild country. But by heading west and then south toward the coast, he'd have less chance of encountering the natives while reaching a port where he could meet with those he sought.

MacKenzie's search for a trail would thus begin on the west bank of the river.

As it happened, the *Raven* would now be going to Pensacola too—something Tyrone wasn't likely to have guessed. In the morning MacKenzie would share his thoughts with Kirkland so that if worst came to worst, they might seize the fugitive before he could meet with the British.

But he'd absolutely no intention of letting matters get that far. Every minute his daughter spent with that man, she'd face danger and brutal treatment. The sooner he was able to locate their trail and find them, the sooner he could bring all that to an end.

After a long time, he slept.

When his eyes reopened, he found that the cabin was still dark. Yet he sensed the day was no longer far off. And he lacked the patience to stay abed in any case.

He sat up, found his boots where he'd left them next to the bunk, and pulled them on. Then he got to his feet and took his jacket from its hook by the entrance. He slipped his arms into it as he stepped out onto the deck.

The moon was down now, but a myriad of stars lightened the cloudless sky, and he found his way easily to the hatch that led down to the compartment where he'd left his weapons.

He recovered the rifle he'd carried earlier and went about checking its load in the light from a low-burning lantern. While he was at this, he heard a noise and looked up with surprise to see that Michael O'Shaughnessy had entered the compartment.

The Irishman did not speak but only favored MacKenzie with a sly glance as he made his way to the weapons locker. He took out the rapier he'd had on the trip to the Indian village and slung its baldric over his shoulder. Then he removed a pistol and started to load it.

MacKenzie watched him in silence for several minutes. But when the other had shoved the pistol into the sash at his waist and hung a powder horn from his free shoulder, he was no longer able to contain his curiosity.

"Now what is it that y're plannin' to do wi' all that deadly equipage y've taken upon y'rself? Are y' meanin' to start a war?"

"Start one?" O'Shaughnessy raised an eyebrow and looked at him with his head tilted to one side. "T' my way o' thinkin', there is already one begun."

"An' who might that war be with?"

"Dread Jamie Tyrone, o' course. He's taken it upon himself to declare war on this vessel an' all her company." He eyed MacKenzie for another moment and then grinned.

"An' a fine war it may promise to be, though not so great in numbers as some I've known. I could not allow myself to let such a one pass, it bein' the only war to hand. So I'd a thought I'd just come along wi' you an' look for a hand in the fightin'."

MacKenzie couldn't speak for several long seconds. His surprise was so great that he failed to notice O'Shaughnessy's use of the appellation "Dread Jamie Tyrone." It was a nickname neither he nor the former pirate had ever used in the other man's presence.

When he finally managed to find his tongue, all he could say at that moment was a terse and mildly disparaging "You?"

"I" came the lofty reply. "*Sarjento* Michael Patrick O'Shaughnessy o' the illustrious Regimento Hibernia." He gave a slight shrug. "Retired."

MacKenzie was staring at him with a mixture of skepticism and disbelief. O'Shaughnessy realized it and nodded.

"I can well imagine what it is you're likely thinkin'. Nor could I find it in myself just now to take so great an exception to it."

He crossed to a built-in bench against the wall where he sat and motioned for MacKenzie to join him. "Take a place beside me here for a bit. This will bear a particle o' explainin'."

After a moment's hesitation, MacKenzie came and took a seat on the bench. A suspicious frown still darkened his face.

"Y' see," O'Shaughnessy said, "I must first confess to a small amount o' fraud aboard this ship an' at the *Castillo*. Now as it happens, all that I related o' my past is true enough. I am a proud veteran o' His Catholic Majesty's armies, both here in the Floridas an' across the water.

"But regardin' all the rest o' it, me bein' pensioned off an' no longer o' service to my king an' country while spendin' my remainin' days as a hopeless an' thick-tongued toper, well, that's not exactly the way o' things. The last was merely a touch o' the play-actin' on my part." He grinned. "Mostly."

If he hoped for a smile from MacKenzie in return, he didn't get it.

"I' truth," he went on with a shrug, "I have never left the Spaniards' employ. I was placed in that cell at the *Castillo* a-purpose: First to keep a secret watch over Dread Jamie Tyrone, whose past transgressions an' questionable loyalties have long been known to us. An' then to discover the facts regardin' your own confinement. The charges against you were a fiction, as was soon apparent. But who an' what might lie behind them was not yet clear."

MacKenzie was listening closely now. He had no wish to interrupt.

"Part o' the answer," O'Shaughnessy continued, "was given by our young lieutenant on that very first night. It was his gold—or that o' his government—which paid for the deception. But why the American navy had covertly entered our sovereign nation was still not known. An' you may well imagine the sort o' worries an' concerns its presence might cause.

"'T was a bit o' good fortune, then, that I was made to come off to sea along wi' you. For I soon discovered the truth. An' this was confirmed by attendin' that meetin' wi' the natives. I could see that it is the British an' not the Americans who are to be feared at the present. The only remainin' difficulty was how I might be able to communicate what I'd learned to the dons."

O'Shaughnessy paused, then shrugged. "It appears the matter may now be about resolvin' itself without any pressin' need to do that. Providin' our Jamie Tyrone can be kept from any hoped-for meetin' wi' the British."

MacKenzie eyed the other man narrowly for a long moment before he responded. "So," he said, "it is now y'r thinkin' to accompany me in my search for Tyrone so you may prevent him from achievin' such a juncture."

"That has entered my mind, yes." O'Shaughnessy nodded. "But there is equally the plight o' your lovely young daughter. I could never stay idly by while she's left to the tender mercies o' that black-hearted villain!"

MacKenzie studied the man beside him for a minute or two longer. Then he said darkly, "So now y' have told me y'r reasons. But y' must yet explain to me what mine should be for acceptin' y'r company on my trek through the wilderness."

"It might just possibly be," O'Shaughnessy replied with a smile, "that even a man like yourself might need some assistance soon or late. I am no stranger to a shindy, as you've cause to know. An' I've a bit o' skill wi' these weapons after my many long years i' the auld regiment. Nor would it be amiss," he added, "to have a second pair o' eyes on your back when followin' after a treacherous dog like Tyrone.

"What might be equally to the point," he concluded with a shrug, "is that I'd be o' no use at all to these Americans were I to stay on aboard here. I' God's truth, I could not tell you what is the difference between a spinnaker an' a sheet!"

MacKenzie remained thoughtfully silent for several long minutes. At last he nodded.

"Well enough. I do believe y' display the qualities o' a fightin' man. An' wi' all that soldierin', I reckon y' shouldn't be entirely helpless on a long trek afoot. So if that is your wish, then come along an' welcome!"

He held out his hand, and a grinning O'Shaughnessy took it.

19

Becky awoke, shivering, to the smell of pines and damp earth. When her eyes opened, she didn't need to look far for the source of either one. She was huddled on the ground at one side of a clearing, partly covered by pine needles that she'd burrowed under for what small warmth they could provide. They clung to her hair and pricked at her face as she struggled to sit up.

Her wrists were tied behind her, and her ankles were bound as well. She'd been lying under the wide-spreading limbs of a huge live oak next to a forest of tall pines. One branch of the tree, thicker than her waist, extended over her head.

During the previous day's journey, James Tyrone had secured another, longer rope about her neck and shoulders so he could use its free end to pull her along after him. *Just like a dog on a leash*, she thought bitterly. When they'd finally stopped for the night, he'd refastened that rope to the cords at her wrists and looped it over the limb of the live oak, knotting it there well outside her reach.

Only after he'd done this and bound her ankles together did he seem to feel safe leaving his slim young captive alone while he went across the clearing and wrapped himself in his cloak to stretch out for his own night's slumber.

He'd left enough slack in the overhead tether to allow her some slight freedom of movement. But she'd no chance at all of leaving this spot or coming anywhere close to him.

Becky's limbs were stiff from the cold and the immobility caused by her bonds, as well as the long trek the previous day. They'd trudged for miles through dense forests and across low rolling hills that had seemed without number. Her captor had clearly been anxious to put as much distance as possible between them and the anchorage where they'd left the *Raven*. He'd probably be forging ahead still if darkness and exhaustion hadn't finally brought him to a grudging halt.

He was no longer a young man, and she could be grateful for that at least. The day's journey had worn her out too, in spite of her youth and what she'd always believed to be her boundless reserves of energy.

She looked up through the branches at the pale morning sky. It was several hours past dawn now. She'd slept late, and a glance at Tyrone's huddled form indicated her captor had yet to awaken.

Her mouth felt like it was full of cotton, and she was terribly thirsty. Her stomach was complaining too. But all such needs would have to depend on her warder's will and convenience. And none would be met until after he'd finally roused himself and seen to his own personal desires.

He had allowed her to drink from time to time during their travels the day before, sprawled on her belly at streams they crossed to lap up water like the dog he seemed to think she was. He'd even spared her a few crusts of bread from the meager supply of provisions he'd taken off the schooner.

It could have been worse, she supposed. But she wasn't so naive as to believe those small considerations were inspired by pity or generosity. Tyrone simply meant to keep her alive. For purposes of his own, which she was firmly resolved not to dwell upon.

She made an effort to push herself several feet along the ground on her backside so as to take advantage of a few warming rays of the sun. Then she decided to take her mind off her discomforts by trying to decide how far they had come during the previous day. And to guess where they were now.

She knew from watching the sky that their general direction had been to the west-southwest. But what distance they'd covered was much harder to estimate.

It had been shortly before noon when Tyrone assaulted the two sailors and then surprised her in the galley. He'd wasted no time or scruples in making a complete search of her person and relieving her of the dirk she once had threatened him with.

After he'd tied her up, he brought the longboat around to ferry them over to the western shore. Once that had been set adrift, he'd spent another few minutes rearranging her bonds so he could lead her up the bank and set out across the country.

From the time he'd first appeared in the galley until they began to make their way through the woods, it had not been more than an hour and possibly less. During the rest of the afternoon they'd trudged along at a steady pace until the winter sky had nearly faded to black. At this season, that would mean five or six hours. With the dense forest and the hilly terrain, they could have traveled a dozen miles.

Or more. Or less. Becky scowled and shook her head, admitting to herself that, in point of fact, she had no idea.

Nor did it matter very much in her present circumstances. She'd no choice right now but to follow wherever her captor led, and for however far he meant to take her. Her calculations had been little more than a way of passing the time and diverting her mind.

Well, no, that wasn't entirely true. She also wanted to guess how long it might be until her father could catch up with them. She'd no doubt at all he would be in pursuit, using all the tracker's skills she knew he possessed. It depended only on how long it had taken him to return to the schooner and then to discover what Tyrone had done.

It was this thought that must sustain her in the days ahead to give her the will and the strength to endure.

Speaking of endurance, there was one other small thing she could apply herself to at the moment. She bent forward at the waist and stretched her arms out behind her, taking several minutes to work her fingers and twist her wrists against the rope that bound them. She'd been doing that whenever she had the chance ever since yesterday afternoon. It always caused pain, for the hemp fibers were sharp and the binding was tight.

She had learned from bitter experience that this would do nothing to loosen the bonds and free her hands. But she intended to keep as much circulation in her extremities as possible so that if Tyrone should ever grow careless, she might seize a weapon or other implement to cut the ropes or make an attack.

She gritted her teeth against the pain as the fibers clawed her flesh, but she persisted in the effort to bring full feeling back to her fingers. And as she moved them to and fro, they chanced to brush lightly against a corner of fabric she'd had tucked up her sleeve. She'd almost forgotten it was there.

It was a lace handkerchief that had once belonged to her mother—practically the only truly feminine item she still kept about her. She'd put it there for the memories it evoked instead of any useful purpose. It made her feel closer to someone she'd lost when she was still a child.

She hadn't given it any thought since leaving the *Raven*—out of sight, out of mind. And until this moment, out of reach as well. But it seemed the stretching and twisting of her arms had gradually worked it downward.

It occurred to her that if she could manage to get it between her fingers and pull it out, she might wrap it around her wrist and get a small amount of relief from those scourging fibers of the hemp.

And then she had another idea.

"Well, now!"

Becky raised her eyes to see the grinning face of James Tyrone, who had come up to stand behind her.

"All bright eyed an' lively feelin' now, are we? Did we enjoy a pleasant night's repose?"

She simply glared at him, swallowing the angry retort that threatened to burst forth.

"Well, lively or not, it's time we two resumed our woodland pilgrimage." He glanced at the sun. "Somewhat past time to my way o' thinkin'. By now there could be others behind who've a thought to come an' join us."

No "could be" about it, Becky thought. She knew her father was bound to follow. And she knew that whatever day he managed to "join them" would be a very bad day indeed for one James Tyrone.

Unless, she told herself grimly, she could somehow find a way to free herself and get her hands upon him first!

The moment he turned to go recover his cloak and other belongings, she was spurred to stealthy but frantic action. She watched from the corners of her eyes as he took a bit of food from his small pack and munched it while slinging the pack over his shoulder. Then he took up the sword and pistol he'd gotten from the *Raven* and belted them on so they'd be ready to hand in case of need.

All the while Becky's fingers were fumbling and stretching desperately in an effort to grasp and pull the kerchief from her sleeve. She bit her lip and tried to keep the strain from showing on her face.

But there was not much need for the last. Tyrone had his back to her until he'd thrown the cloak about himself and fastened it at his chest. When he turned around, he held a small piece of bread in his hand.

He grinned and crossed the clearing to where she was sitting. Instead of freeing her hands, he indicated by a gesture that she should open her mouth. Then, holding the bread at arm's length, he bent, thrust it quickly between her teeth, and jerked his hand back—for all the world as if she were some feral animal.

While she chewed, Tyrone knelt and untied her ankles. She watched him contemptuously but wasted no energy on a pointless attempt to kick or struggle. At the moment her legs and feet were numb from the bonds.

He stepped away and reached up to unfasten the rope from the tree limb. Becky got stiffly to her feet and backed toward the bole of the live oak. When Tyrone approached to once more loop his "leash" around her neck, her shoulders were almost touching the rough bark.

Tyrone took up the slack and made a wide detour around her to exit the western edge of the clearing. "All right, my beauty!" he said, giving the rope a sharp tug. "Once more unto the breach!"

Becky stumbled at first. But she quickly recovered her balance and submissively followed her captor into the forest.

He didn't spare her another look until they were well among the trees. When he finally glanced back, she managed to suppress the smile that tugged at the corners of her lips.

A hurried look over her shoulder as they were leaving the clearing had given her a parting glimpse of the great oak that dominated all its surroundings. Fluttering lightly in the morning breeze was a lacy white handkerchief, its corner thrust into a narrow crack in the bark that she'd pulled apart with her fingers.

It was a sight that could not fail to draw the eye of anyone who came within a dozen yards of it.

20

An early morning fog made finding any trail Tyrone and his captive might have left on the west bank of the Apalachicola a challenging prospect. But MacKenzie was unwilling to delay the start of his quest for even an hour. As soon as it was light enough to make out the shapes of the trees, he asked that a boat be lowered to take O'Shaughnessy and himself ashore.

In addition to weapons, powder horns, and pouches of lead balls, each wore a light haversack containing food for several days and other items such as spare flints, dry tinder, and a few useful tools. To ward off the cold, MacKenzie had on his buckskin jacket, while around O'Shaughnessy's shoulders was a woolen cloak.

Their food consisted of hard biscuits and strips of dried beef that MacKenzie had gotten from the Indians. The Spanish called this food *charqui*, but the word had become "jerky" to Americans on the frontier. MacKenzie thought it much more palatable than salt pork, and it needed no lengthy soaking or cooking in order to make it edible. They each carried a water bottle as well, for those times when they might not be near a river or stream.

All of this made for a bit of a burden, but not enough of one to hinder swift progress through the woodlands. And it was far less than O'Shaughnessy had often been laden down with in his service with the Spanish army.

As soon as they debarked on the sandy, rock-strewn riverbank, MacKenzie turned south and began carefully scanning the area for tracks. He advanced slowly and knelt often, his eyes shifting constantly with periodic glances at the nearest undergrowth for disturbances that might reveal the passage of a man and a woman. Despite his strong sense of urgency, no purpose would be served by careless haste, which risked overlooking some small and vital clue.

O'Shaughnessy followed a few steps behind, clutching his cloak tightly against the damp chill of the fog and an icy breeze that came off the water. The sun was still well below the high eastern bluffs.

He watched MacKenzie with curious interest but asked no questions and ventured no comments—not even when his companion paused to examine something on the ground that he himself couldn't see and could not even guess at. He understood he was in the presence of an expert tracker, and he'd no wish to distract him or make a nuisance of himself in any way.

His ears caught the sounds of activity aboard the *Raven*, and when he looked in that direction, he could see the schooner's anchor was being weighed and a sail shaken out. A few minutes later she had gotten under way, and before very much longer she had disappeared from sight around a bend in the river.

If MacKenzie was conscious of this departure, he gave no sign.

They continued to make their way slowly downstream, with nothing being found to show where Tyrone and his prisoner could have left the river. After perhaps a mile of meticulous searching, MacKenzie looked back at his companion and shook his head. He turned and started to retrace his steps.

The fog had begun to lift now, and he kept to his unhurried progress, his attention still on the ground and the woods to his left. His scrutiny as they returned to their landing place seemed at least as intent as it had been before.

They passed that spot, marked by furrows where the boat had come ashore, and continued upstream at the same deliberate pace. Several hundred yards beyond it, there was a densely wooded section of the bank where the trees extended down to the water and the ground next to the river was low and boggy.

MacKenzie slowed his pace and searched the area here even more closely.

Suddenly he uttered a grunt and knelt by a muddy place a few inches from the river. He examined this narrowly for a moment, then turned his eyes to the jumble of vines and thick undergrowth on his left.

He nodded and looked back at O'Shaughnessy. "'T was here they came ashore," he said. "An' no mistakin'." He waved his companion closer and pointed to a few muddy depressions that were partly filled with water. "Two heavy boot prints yonder an' two smaller ones behind."

He turned to indicate the woods that extended up a slight rise from the river. "An' they left us few questions regardin' where they went after."

Even O'Shaughnessy could easily make out the ragged path of broken branches and trodden-down shrubs that led away from the bank.

"Tyrone's no woodsman, I reckon." MacKenzie stood and bent down to brush the mud from his breeches. "An' there's little doubt he felt a pressin' need for haste into the bargain. He took no pains at all to hide their passin'."

He straightened and shook his head. "Had we started our lookin' this way upstream instead o' down, we'd no' ha' missed the trail this long hour past. Yet wi' the river's current I believed the other the more likely."

He brushed off his hands and shrugged. "But what is done is done. An' now we have finally found our direction." He glanced at the sky. "Wi' the day still young enough for some miles o' travel!"

O'Shaughnessy nodded agreement and looked back over his shoulder to where the sun was just making its appearance above the eastern bluffs. When he turned his eyes again toward his companion all he could see were the broad shoulders of MacKenzie's buckskin jacket as they disappeared among the trees.

He made haste to follow but quickly found himself harassed and delayed by the thick tangled growth that bordered the river. Numerous roots and vines clutched at his feet, and low-growing limbs appeared to leap up before his eyes. As often as not, these last were encircled by creepers or cobwebs. O'Shaughnessy muttered a silent curse at the spiteful Nature who seemed to have equipped every plant in Florida with sharp-pointed spurs or venomous thorns.

Nor did it help that the ground was rising steadily as they made their way farther from the water.

None of it seemed to slow MacKenzie's long-striding pace. He could be glimpsed some yards ahead, stepping over or pushing aside all obstructions in his path. Nor did he spare time for any backward glances. It seemed he just assumed the other would follow. Or perhaps, O'Shaughnessy was beginning to think, he didn't much care whether he did or he didn't.

He struggled on but could tell he was falling farther behind. He was starting to fear he might be abandoned to find his own way through this devilish wilderness. It was with a weary sigh of relief that he emerged from yet another dense thicket to find that his companion had at last come to a halt.

The frontiersman was kneeling beside a small stream, studying its bank with a dark scowl. O'Shaughnessy had to pause for a moment with his hands on his knees until he'd recovered his breath enough to approach him.

"He's got her all bound up wi' ropes," MacKenzie growled when the other came near. "Draggin' her behind like a shoat to the market!"

O'Shaughnessy was still a bit winded, and it was another minute before he could respond, "'T would seem to prove, though, that she remains among the livin'. An' that at least is a very great blessin'."

"Aye. Or yesterday she was. An' keepin' pace wi' the villain stride for stride. They were makin' rapid progress, so there's hope he's no' had time to do her any greater mischief."

"D' you think we'd now be about closin' the distance between us?"

"'T is too early to tell. But never doubt that we shall, the Almighty willin' and human strength bein' constant." He got to his feet. "Their trail is still plain enough. Yonder through the trees."

He pointed. But O'Shaughnessy saw no trail, plain or otherwise. He simply nodded and took another deep breath. Then he did his best to match his companion's long stride as they crossed the creek and started off through the trees.

21

Several hours later and quite a few miles to the south, Jeremiah and John Robert MacKenzie spurred their mounts to the top of a grassy hill where they could at last look down on the broad, dark waters of the Apalachicola.

"Well, brother of mine"—Jeremiah took a foot out of the stirrup and rested it over his saddle—"we've found us the big river. Now what do we do?"

John Robert frowned and didn't answer immediately. He studied the water and the wooded banks on either side for a minute or two. Then he shook his head. "I'm not rightly sure where we'd best be goin' from here. But I reckon if this river was where those Yankees was headin', an' if it was in their minds to meet up with some Creeks, they'd prob'ly find a heap more of 'em somewheres to the north. Maybe that's the direction we'd ought to start lookin'."

"Good a plan as any, I reckon." Jeremiah shrugged. "But I sure do wish we'd got some better notion of what it was they were thinkin'."

"Spaniards didn't 'pear to have any better idea 'bout that than we do. Less, I reckon. 'Least we heard that navy feller make his case to Pa when he asked for his help."

"Uh-huh. You think he knew what-all he was talkin' 'bout back there? 'Bout the Brits plannin' to stir up the Injuns an' then land a bunch of their troops?"

"Maybe. Sounded pretty sure of what he was sayin', anyhow. An' if he was right, we need to step mighty careful our own selves, wanderin' 'round up yonder in Creek country."

"Trouble of it is, they'd be the best ones to ask where Pa an' them others could be right now. Nothin' too much happens in their lands they ain't seen or heard tell of."

"Well, maybe there's still a couple friendly ones 'round an' about. If we can manage to find 'em an' talk to 'em without gettin' our hair lifted."

They fell silent and let the horses rest for several more minutes. Then they lifted the reins and started them walking toward the north.

Jeremiah suddenly pulled up short and twisted his body in the saddle. "Hold on a second! You see that?"

"What?" John Robert brought his mount alongside and looked where his brother was pointing.

A sleek two-masted schooner had appeared from behind a bend in the river, gliding slowly downstream with the current. A few small sails showed at the bow and the topmast.

Jeremiah shaded his eyes against the afternoon sun. "You reckon that there is the boat those Americans made off with?"

"More'n likely, I expect. How many boats that size you figure there'd be on this lonely stretch of river?"

"Well, let's go down yonder an' fetch her!" Jeremiah swung his horse's head around and started for the grassy slope that led to the river's bank. John Robert reached over and grabbed his reins.

"Hold on now an' just think for a minute! I know these here animals are right good swimmers. But they ain't about to catch up to some sailboat in the water. An' in case you didn't notice it right yet, she's got her some kind of a cannon mounted yonder on the deck."

Jeremiah pulled up, still staring at the schooner. "So what is it you 'magine we're gonna do?"

"We'll just follow along for a piece an' keep our eyes on her. We don't know for sure right now it's the same boat or, if it is, whether they still got Pa on it with 'em. Might be he managed to get away from 'em somehow." John Robert paused, then went on more slowly. "Even if it's the one we're lookin' for an' he's there on board, we got us some careful figurin' to do before we go tryin' to help him."

The part of the Apalachicola they could see from their vantage point ran straight for almost a mile. They followed along the bluff and down through an open pine forest where for a time they could watch the schooner and activities on her deck without any difficulty.

But then the river began a series of twists and curves, its banks thickly forested or bordered by low-lying swamps. The brothers were forced to make frequent detours, riding inland for a distance and then finding their way back to some place where they could again view the water and the vessel without impediment. Yet there was little chance of fully losing track of the *Raven*. Her tall masts could readily be seen from a distance, in stark silhouette against the sky.

From what they'd observed in the course of several hours, they now knew this was indeed the ship they'd been seeking. Lieutenant Kirkland was easily recognized as he stood at the helm, a post he'd not once been seen to leave. A couple of his crew were in evidence as well, though their numbers seemed fewer than might have been expected.

. Of their father there had been absolutely no sign at all. Either he wasn't on the ship or he was confined someplace inside it. There was no way to guess which it was from a distance. And of course that knowledge was vital to whatever they decided to do next.

After trudging along for half a day, it became abundantly clear to O'Shaughnessy and MacKenzie what the two they pursued had already learned: this country to the west of the Apalachicola was not nearly so flat as they might earlier have supposed. It lacked the craggy bluffs and rock-bound ravines they'd had to cope with on their way to the Indian village. But the seemingly endless series of gently rolling hills—not obvious at first because of the dense growth along the river—in time made their trek every bit as taxing as that previous journey.

Most of the hills were covered by forests of tall pines whose shade encouraged few plants to grow beneath them. This made for somewhat easier walking, and the general lack of brambles or thorny vines was especially pleasing to O'Shaughnessy.

It wasn't always the case when they descended a slope to one of the numerous winding creeks that needed to be crossed. But usually the junglelike growth that bordered them was no more than a few yards wide. And the Irishman decided that if these were the worst impediments he encountered for the rest of the journey, he might just be able to keep up with his companion in the future.

He might. And then again, he might not.

MacKenzie seemed determined to set a relentless pace, uphill and downhill, showing little regard for the contours of the terrain and pausing only occasionally for a brief study of the ground. He spoke rarely, and O'Shaughnessy stayed silent as well, trudging grimly along beside or behind the frontiersman as their forest surroundings permitted.

There were times, off and on, when the dense woodland yielded abruptly to wide, grassy savanna, mostly shades of yellowish brown now under the winter sun. Often these stretched for several miles into the distance. Yet, whenever the travelers made it to the top of one of those low barren knolls, they always saw another dark-green ribbon of woodland awaiting them on the horizon.

The unbroken landscape of forested hills seemed to go on forever.

At last MacKenzie called for a midday halt in a small clearing among the pines. When he spoke, O'Shaughnessy thought he detected a little shortness of breath in his companion's clipped words. And once he'd taken a seat on a fallen log, the man's broad shoulders seemed to sag a bit before he reached for his water bottle.

It came as a mild surprise, for until then the frontiersman had seemed almost like some tireless automaton not subject to human frailty. O'Shaughnessy frankly couldn't help but view this revelation with a touch of relief. He was feeling more than a little worn out himself. Only pride and thoughts of being left behind again had kept him from speaking of it.

He sat on the ground with his back to a tree and took out his own water bottle for a long drink. He studied his companion without speaking for several minutes.

Then he said quietly, "It is a long journey that still lies ahead o' us. An' the nature o' this up an' down country is not kind to a man's legs."

MacKenzie fetched a strip of jerky from his pack and didn't reply.

"Just speakin' for myself only, I am beginnin' to feel just a small touch o' weariness already."

MacKenzie took a bite of the jerky and started to chew. Still he said nothing.

"Do you not think," the Irishman persisted, "that we might p'rhaps do better proceedin' like two long-distance runners instead o' some headlong sprinters? We'll neither o' us do any good service to your daughter should we fall by the wayside wi' the race not yet finished."

The only response he got from his companion was a glance and a disparaging grunt.

O'Shaughnessy shrugged and let the matter drop. He'd had his say, and there seemed nothing else to do. He took some jerky from his own pack and chewed it in silence.

When they'd finished their sparse meal, they drank again from their water bottles and then got stiffly to their feet. MacKenzie set out as resolutely as before with O'Shaughnessy grimly matching his pace.

Yet they had not gone far before the Irishman nodded and smiled to himself. His single-minded companion—whether by willing choice or not—was now taking his advice.

22

Throughout the long trek, the hills and the unyielding wilderness were taking their toll on James Tyrone as well. Becky noticed that he'd been stopping to rest more often. Sometimes he'd just lean against a tree for a minute or two to catch his breath. But other times he'd find a seat on a fallen log or on the pine-needle-covered earth and remain unmoving for as much as half an hour.

These were hopeful signs, for they showed the older man's desperate energy of the day before was starting to flag. And every such delay would give her father more time to close the distance between them.

Not that it had provided her any chance for escape as yet. Tyrone was relentlessly careful when they halted to keep his distance and never took his eyes off her. Nor had he shown the least inclination to ease the bonds that rendered her helpless.

But she believed the periods of rest were doing her more good than they were her captor. With the resilience of youth, she'd begun to feel less exhausted than she had the day before and so better prepared to face whatever trials still lay ahead.

She also had hopes that those signs of tiring on Tyrone's part meant the one trial she'd most been fearing would be postponed for at least another night and perhaps for longer.

The extended halts in their journey had also given her the opportunity at times to leave behind small clues to their presence and expected route of travel: a twig or a knotted tuft of grass bent to point the way or a pile of pebbles with another at the side to show direction.

She'd had to be careful to hide these markers from Tyrone, so none could be located where they'd readily draw attention. They might easily be overlooked by a casual observer. But she knew from lifelong experience that in the Florida wilderness, John Thomas MacKenzie was not a man whom anyone could describe as casual.

Tyrone called a halt for the night well before dark this time, in the midst of a forest of tall pines with only sporadic undergrowth. Again Becky's feet were bound together; then her "leash" was tied at her wrists and secured high up around the rough bole of one of the larger trees. This left her with scarcely enough freedom to lie down and make her solitary bed among the scattered needles on the ground.

Her captor said hardly a word as he went about those tasks. His cheery banter of the morning seemed to have entirely deserted him.

Nor did he offer her anything to eat tonight. And as far as she could tell, he took nothing for his own supper. He merely trudged over to a spot some dozen yards away and carelessly dropped his pack and weapons on the ground. Then he flung his body down beside them with his cloak about his shoulders. Within minutes she could hear his snoring.

Becky listened to it for a time, considering. But in her present helpless state she could find no advantage in his mindless slumber. She might try gnawing at the rope that held her to the tree. But even if that succeeded, her feet would still be tied together. And if she could somehow manage to get those free as well, her hands were bound behind her. It all seemed to promise nothing but an exhausting waste of effort.

It made far better sense, she decided, to take advantage of the long hours until daylight to get as much rest and sleep for herself as possible. At some future time, with luck, there would be other opportunities.

She relaxed her body and closed her eyes. And without further concerns, she slept.

Although he had indeed tried to pace himself more sensibly through the long afternoon, MacKenzie kept pushing relentlessly on until the fading light in the forest made it almost impossible to find their way. By that time he could feel a heavy weariness in his legs and shoulders, and he knew without asking that O'Shaughnessy must be at least as fatigued. He felt a growing respect for the Irishman, who kept plodding resolutely along beside him without malingering or complaint.

They halted near a small stand of low-growing hardwoods, and despite his weariness, MacKenzie went about building a crude shelter in the gathering dusk by bending down branches and covering them with palmetto fronds he cut from a nearby thicket.

O'Shaughnessy watched him curiously, his offer of help having been politely refused. And it was clear his companion had no need of it, for the entire task from start to finish took no more than a quarter of an hour. He was impressed by the accomplishment but wondered why MacKenzie had troubled to do it at all. The sky had remained clear and almost free of clouds throughout the entire day.

"The weather is ever an uncertain thing in this Florida country," he was told when he asked. "A sudden tempest may descend upon us at any time, very oft when it's least expected. The cost o' bein' prepared for such a thing is small, an' 't is more than worth the trouble."

They made their beds from pine boughs pulled under the shelter, then ate a hasty meal of hardtack and jerky with "Adam's ale" to slake their thirst. Afterward both stretched out their tired bodies as comfortably as possible and wasted little time in falling to sleep.

Darkness brought with it a chill northerly breeze. But there was to be no warming campfire. Although he believed the chance was slight, MacKenzie was unwilling to take the risk that Tyrone might still be near enough to see or smell one. They had no real way to guess how far the fugitive and his prisoner might have managed to come through this unfamiliar wilderness.

And, of course, there were always the Indians.

The MacKenzie brothers kept up their pursuit of the schooner until the sun had descended behind the trees. Then they watched while the *Raven*'s small crew took in its few sails and dropped anchor in midstream.

The river's bank opposite the ship here was low and grassy with few trees close to the water. Jeremiah and John Robert had reined in their mounts several dozen yards away, concealed by the leafy shadows of a stand of hardwoods. They spoke in whispers, knowing well how easily sound can travel over water and in the still evening air.

"What you think?" Jeremiah said. "You reckon Pa's still on that boat?"

"Maybe. Could be they got him locked up inside it somewheres." John Robert shook his head. "But it's not 'pearin' so likely to me as it did a couple hours ago. Question is, how can we go about makin' sure if he is or he isn't?"

"Only one way I can think of." Jeremiah swung down from his saddle. "Let's you an' me just rest up a bit 'til it comes on full dark. Then I me got a notion to have a li'l moonlight swim."

John Robert looked at him, then shrugged and dismounted. He decided his brother was right. They'd not seen their father on board for the entire afternoon. Waiting and watching for even longer on the off chance he might appear could just be time wasted with no useful result. And time was something they needed to be thinking about as the schooner got closer to the open Gulf.

Jeremiah was a fine swimmer, the best in the family except possibly for Becky. And he was able to move through the water with barely a sound or a ripple. Whether he could manage to get on board the ship, with barnacles along the hull and no good handholds, was a different matter. But if it could be done, he would do it, with silence and stealth in the process.

They made themselves comfortable under the trees and ate a light supper of cold biscuits and jerky, sharing little conversation while they waited for the sky to turn black and the sounds of activity on the schooner to gradually grow less.

At last it was quiet and only one man was on watch. They could see that he made periodic rounds of the deck, but these were not frequent and took little time to complete. Mostly he stayed aft with his back resting against the binnacle. To John Robert and Jeremiah, observing him from a distance, his thoughts seemed to be elsewhere. Possibly he was drowsing.

When he'd become familiar with the sailor's routine, Jeremiah stripped down to his underwear and left the trees for the river. He slipped noiselessly into the water while John Robert watched. His dark form could be seen slowly gliding toward the schooner. But then it was lost against the blackness of the hull.

More than an hour passed before he finally reappeared.

He emerged shivering from the water and was met by his brother with a blanket that was quickly wrapped about his shoulders. He clutched it to himself and gave John Robert a meaningful look but said nothing until they'd returned to the stand of trees where they'd left their horses and his clothes.

"Mighty big news," he said quietly as he put on his hat and undid the reins. "Let's get a li'l distance behind us to where we can build a fire without anybody noticin' it." He gathered his clothes and swung into the saddle, still in his underwear with the blanket over his shoulders.

John Robert would have been much happier to find out what the "big news" about their father was right then and there. But before he could even ask a question, Jeremiah had reined his mount around and started it moving away from the river at a fast walk.

He hurried to untie the rest of the horses and get himself into the saddle. There was nothing else he could do at the moment but follow along behind and try to guess what it was that Jeremiah had learned.

23

During their two-day voyage downstream, the small crew of the *Raven* had suffered none of the exhausting effects of terrain that plagued the other travelers in West Florida, even though the number of miles they'd covered was enormously greater. Yet the endless hours aboard ship had been stressful and wearying in their own way.

Kirkland had remained at the helm for almost the entire time, never speaking except when it was necessary to issue infrequent commands. His face was fixed in a dark scowl that warned Sergeant Jaynes and the others to keep their distance unless on the most urgent of ship's business. They could see their captain was deeply troubled and were wise enough to know this had less to do with any danger from the Indians or the British than the fate of a certain young woman many miles to the north.

The somber mood aboard ship was not improved when word was passed that their injured shipmate had drawn his final breath sometime during the night.

The brief evening visit by Jeremiah had gone unnoticed. Swimming in a circle around the schooner, he'd found no ready way to climb aboard. But as it turned out, he'd had no need.

When he approached the bow, he was able to hear clearly the sailors in the fo'c's'le as they talked among themselves. All that was required was to tread water for a time in order to learn what he wanted to know about his father and much else besides: the unexpected presence of his sister, the treachery of Tyrone, and MacKenzie's setting out across country in pursuit.

The *Raven* had weighed anchor early the next morning and by that afternoon had come in sight of the blue-green expanse of Apalachicola Bay. Overall it had taken her fewer hours to return downstream than was needed for her earlier trip north to seek out the Indians. They'd been helped by a brisk northwesterly breeze in addition to the current.

When they reached the river's mouth, Kirkland ordered the anchor lowered while the bodies of the two dead seamen were sewn into canvas and lead weights attached. Once this task was completed and the tide had become favorable, the crew shook out the sails, and they crossed the bay to the pass between St. George and St. Vincent Islands. Here they would once more enter into the open Gulf.

Along the way they saw Indians at a distance, wading among the island shallows or standing upright in dugout canoes. They seemed to be busy gathering oysters or other fruits of the sea and seldom paused to glance in the schooner's direction. Apparently the presence of such vessels in these coastal waters was not that great a novelty.

Their lack of interest or curiosity and the absence of any overt signs of hostility were encouraging signs to the men on the *Raven*.

After they'd reached the Gulf, Kirkland held a course due south for several miles until they could be certain they'd reached deeper water. There the sails were reefed, and preparations were made for bidding a last farewell to their fallen comrades.

The shrouded bodies were laid on planks that jutted out over the rail, covered by sheets in lieu of flags. They'd brought only a single American ensign with them, and this wouldn't be displayed until they entered the harbor at Pensacola. Or perhaps if they chanced to encounter some Spanish vessel along the way.

All those who remained of the crew assembled on deck, and each came to attention while Kirkland read the traditional service for the dead. Then Sergeant Jaynes touched a linstock to the small cannon at the bow, and the ends of the planks were tipped up so that the bodies of the seamen were consigned to the deep.

Everyone saluted as the thunderous roar echoed across the water. And with that the brief ceremony was completed.

Kirkland turned and strode briskly back to the helm. When he'd taken hold of the wheel, he called out loudly to his crew, "Lively now! Lay on every scrap of canvas she will bear! The sooner we reach Pensacola, the sooner there may be time for other matters!"

No one needed to ask what "other matters" he had in his mind. There was still the matter of Becky MacKenzie and her captor, who they all believed was now headed toward the same destination.

Every man leapt to his task, and Kirkland spun the wheel, pointing the *Raven*'s bow at the western horizon.

From St. Vincent Island the Florida coast made a broad sweeping arc, curving west-northwest and then back west-southwest until it came to the pass between barrier islands that would take them into Pensacola Bay. But Kirkland had no intention of hugging the shore all that distance. There were shallows and shoals near land that might put his ship at risk or, at the very least, make the journey longer.

Instead, he meant to set a course due west, navigating by sun and stars until they reached a point where they could turn to the north and make a straight run toward their destination.

He believed this would also give them the best chance of avoiding an encounter with other vessels, either Spanish or—as he'd reason to suspect from the intelligence he'd received—British warships cruising the area on a preinvasion reconnaissance.

The hours slipped past, for the most part uneventfully. The sails were drawing well, and the nimble schooner was not difficult to manage even with the limited crew she now had available.

From time to time contrary winds forced them to tack in order to keep their westerly course, but overall they were making excellent progress. Calculations from casting out the taffrail log showed their speed was averaging between four and five knots. At this rate they would reach Pensacola within another twenty-four hours.

Jeremiah and John Robert were following a northerly course now, riding hard and changing horses every few hours. After Jeremiah's report of what he'd heard from those aboard the schooner, both now knew that their father was no longer on her. Instead, he was somewhere out in the forested wilderness to the west of the Apalachicola in pursuit of a villainous James Tyrone and their captive sister.

Darkness and unfamiliarity with the country had forced them to wait impatiently for daylight before putting their fresh change of plan into action. But ever since that time, they'd been pushing their mounts and themselves with unstinting effort. The trail they meant to seek was already two days old. And they still had no clear idea of how they would go about finding it.

Since no one on the *Raven* had any knowledge of where either the pursued or the pursuers might have gone since the previous day, they must first identify the place upstream where the schooner had anchored and the journey had been made to the Indian village. After that they must cross the river and pick up the trails of their father and the others.

Their tracking skills had been learned from their sire, and they had few doubts that in time they could manage to accomplish all of this. But time was of the essence now, and how much time would be needed was the burning question.

It was a question that nagged at the minds of both brothers throughout the long ride and kept them in their saddles with scant pauses for rest.

MacKenzie and O'Shaughnessy had been up with the sun as well. They wasted no time preparing breakfast, simply chewing on some jerky while they went about demolishing their temporary shelter and spreading its remains about the forest floor. MacKenzie was still mindful of the Indians, though he knew any such small efforts at concealment would accomplish little beyond a short delay if there was a real desire to pursue them. But he always thought it best to do whatever he could to leave wild country in the same state he'd found it.

The shadows before them were still long when they set out once more among the forested hills on the trail of their quarry.

After several hours, they came to a small clearing with a great live oak at one edge. MacKenzie paused there to study their surroundings. Then he began a slow circuit of the place with his eyes on the ground.

"'T was here they tarried for the night," he said after a minute or two. "Tyrone's tracks are all about, an' yonder the grass is crushed down where he lay there asleep." He frowned. "But wi' regard to Rebecca . . ."

His eyes followed some footprints that went to the live oak and back. He approached the tree and looked at the ground, then at the limb overhead.

"Hogtied an' left here all alone, by the Almighty, to find sleep as best she could! An' tethered to that branch yonder into the bargain!" He pointed. "Y' see the scars made by the rope?"

O'Shaughnessy had stayed at the far side of the clearing and doubted he would have noticed the faint marks his companion was indicating even if he'd been next to them.

MacKenzie knelt for a closer examination of the place by the live oak. Suddenly he gave a loud shout and reached out to clutch something that had been lying on the ground.

O'Shaughnessy watched in amazement as the man he'd privately thought of as a dour Scotsman leapt suddenly to his feet and did a fair imitation of an Irish jig. "What in the world is it, man? Have you taken leave o' your senses entirely?"

MacKenzie spun on his heel and waved a sodden piece of cloth above his head. "It is this, by the Lord!"

He brought it over to where O'Shaughnessy could see it. It was a woman's lace handkerchief, wet from the dew and somewhat soiled by a night on the ground.

"It is Rebecca's!" MacKenzie said triumphantly. "An' before that 't was her mother's. She's left it for us as a sign she was here!'"

O'Shaughnessy looked up from the handkerchief and frowned. "'T is not so easily seen a place to leave such a device. Do you think p'rhaps she carelessly lost it instead?"

"Careless? Not my Rebecca! She's little enough left to her that once was her mother's, an' she treasures every item. No, she left it here a-purpose for me to discover!"

He hesitated for a moment and glanced at the great oak. "Although," he said thoughtfully, "it could be she tried fixin' it to yon tree somehow an' the wind or an animal worked it loose so it fell."

He shrugged and then favored O'Shaughnessy with a rare smile. "At all events, she'd me in her thoughts an' contrived to leave somethin' to show she was here. For she'd never a doubt that I'd be comin' after!"

24

The weather on the Gulf remained fair and sunny through most of the afternoon. There were a just few fleecy clouds overhead, drifting slowly off toward the north.

But as the sun dipped lower these began to move more swiftly and separated into ragged streaks as they neared the horizon. The winds grew variable and after a time blew strongly from the south-southwest. The air they brought with them was heavy with moisture and had an oppressive feeling about it. The sailors aboard the *Raven* knew the signs: as so often could happen at these southern latitudes, an unexpected storm was in the offing.

By the time the sun was low in the west, its face could no longer be seen behind tall black thunderheads that seemed to have risen from the sea in a matter of minutes. Lightning flickered fitfully inside the looming mass, accompanied by angry rumbles of thunder.

The water of the Gulf took on a dull and oily color, with long white-capped rollers that buffeted the schooner from side to side. Kirkland was forced to turn her bow into the swells in order to avoid the danger of capsizing.

There was little doubt they were in for a blow, and he'd already ordered the sails to be reefed with just enough canvas on the forward stays to allow the *Raven* to answer the helm. He was doubly thankful as he fought to hold the wheel in the shifting seas that he'd elected to keep to the open water and not risk being trapped against a lee shore.

The full fury of the tempest struck shortly after dark, sweeping the decks with torrential rain and more often than not overflowing the scuppers. The waves rose about them to tremendous heights, surprising in view of the relative shallowness of the Gulf.

Inevitably some of those fell over the ship, halting her forward progress and dragging her down until, at what seemed the last moment, her bow broke free of the swirling black water to offer yet another short-lived promise of survival. The sailors clung to the masts and rigging, desperately resisting the pull of the current until the waters subsided and they could once more take in great gulps of air. And the moment they did, the screaming wind seemed to be trying its best to wrench the breath from their lungs.

It was the age-old battle between man and unbridled nature, one that each man on the *Raven* had fought more than once. They shook off their fears and exhaustion along with the water and went grimly about the tasks of keeping their frail vessel afloat.

Luckily they'd had time to observe the storm's approach and had done all that could be done to secure the ship against the blow. And although violent enough to tax each man to the limit, in the end the ordeal proved to be relatively short lived. After only three or four hours, there remained little beyond a persistent drizzle and the long sweeping combers to remind them of what they'd been forced to endure.

Still, it was fair to say that no one aboard the *Raven* got much sleep during the night. And the dark overcast that followed left them with no way to take their bearings and make a guess at their location until the sky finally cleared sometime the next day.

They increased their sail only slightly once the storm was over. Then Kirkland made an effort to maintain their course toward what he hoped and believed was still the west. This was largely a matter of relying on his seaman's instincts along with more than a few silent prayers.

Between which he cursed bitterly at the unplanned delay.

The storm arrived at the camping place of MacKenzie and O'Shaughnessy some hours later than it had struck on the Gulf.

When they were awakened by a crash of thunder followed by the heavy drumming of rain through the leaves, O'Shaughnessy opened his eyes and said a silent prayer of thanks for his companion's wilderness knowledge and foresight. They were protected from the worst of the deluge by another hasty shelter he'd made, and only a few occasional spates from above plus a smattering of wind-blown drops invaded their resting place.

Still, the wind brought with it a fresh chill to the air, and while it moaned through the trees, they sat up to huddle together under O'Shaughnessy's woolen cloak. This was their only source of warmth in the regrettable absence of a fire.

At least O'Shaughnessy regretted it. MacKenzie seemed to be giving it little or no thought. He sat stoically silent with his arms about his knees while the periodic flashes of lightning revealed a dark scowl on his face.

As had been the case far to the south, the tempest soon moved past them and was followed by a steady drizzle and the soft patter of water dripping from the leaves. They could still hear rumbles of thunder farther off to the north. But in time these grew fewer and more distant, which seemed to confirm that the worst of the storm was over.

O'Shaughnessy offered up another silent prayer of thanks to a benevolent Providence that had spared them from a longer ordeal. But when he pulled aside his cloak so the two men could move apart, he was surprised to learn that MacKenzie didn't appear to share his feelings of relief.

The frontiersman shifted his position to one side of the shelter and then knelt there gazing balefully out at their dark and dripping surroundings. A muttered series of curses could be heard issuing from his lips.

"What is it, man?" O'Shaughnessy spoke from behind him, keeping his own voice low as well. "Surely the storm has passed us by now, wi' neither the worse for wear." He paused, but there was no reply.

He moved a foot or two to one side and craned his neck to peer out from under the covering branches. "An' even now I believe I may detect a faint lightenin' away to the east. There is a warmin' sun i' the prospect, I'm thinkin', an' a fresh-washed sky along wi' it."

MacKenzie still said nothing, but it seemed from behind that his shoulders slumped just a bit.

"An' so what might be the cause o' that surly cursin'?" the Irishman went on. "There is little ahead that I can see to further impede our progress."

"A fresh-washed sky," MacKenzie repeated dully. "Aye, 't is likely enough." He turned toward his companion. "An' a fresh-washed earth as well into the bargain!"

O'Shaughnessy could not see his face in the darkness. But the bitterness in his voice could not be mistaken. "There is no trail remainin' for us to follow, do y' see? That accursed flood o' rain, along wi' the heavy wind that brought it, will ha' washed away now every last track an' other sign o' the two that we are after. Just as clean an' bare as the day this world was created!"

25

James Tyrone, as MacKenzie had observed earlier, was no woodsman. When the storm swept through the clearing where he and Becky had bedded down for the night, there was no man-made shelter and little other protection from the elements.

As it turned out, Becky fared somewhat better than her captor during those first torrential minutes. She'd been secured to the lower trunk of a large magnolia whose broad waxy leaves fended off the worst of the downpour.

Tyrone, on the ground some dozen yards away, rose spluttering and cursing from his slumber and looked wildly around him, momentarily at a loss to know what had happened or how to escape it. Then he shook the water from his eyes and grabbed his hat and cloak to scurry over to the tree where he'd left the young woman.

He crouched there beside her, still swearing savagely and hunching his shoulders against the cold drops. He'd left his rapier and pistol behind in his haste, and Becky, with her hands and feet still tied and no weapon in reach even at such close quarters, felt like cursing herself over what she could only view as a lost opportunity.

After few minutes, Tyrone became conscious of their nearness and moved several feet away while still not leaving the cover of the sheltering branches. He ceased his tirade when he did this, but in the blackness between them she could still hear his ragged breathing brought on by his earlier exertions.

Slowly this became less, and then for a long time she heard nothing at all besides the sound of the drumming rain.

She'd no way of guessing what the man next to her might be doing or planning during that extended period of darkness. It made her uneasy and—she confessed to herself—more than a little afraid. She found herself holding her body rigid in anticipation of a possible assault, though in her present helpless state she knew any hope of resistance was slight.

But there was no attack. Tyrone maintained his distance, such as it was. And when the rain finally slackened and the storm began to move past, she heard his calm unruffled voice coming from where he'd apparently been all the while.

"Well, the tempest will soon be spent now, I'm thinkin'. Wi' the two o' us sufferin' no grievous harm." Becky almost thought she could hear a smile behind his words. "'T was after all but a momentary exigency in the great broad scheme o' things."

He was silent again for a time while the rain subsided and the forest seemed to grow still. "An' now," he said, "I do believe I detect a slight trace o' gray in the heavens there to eastward. The new day comes on us apace!"

There was a rustling in the leaves as Tyrone rose to his feet. "I must go to recover my property from where I abandoned it i' the storm. 'T will require a bit o' time for me to clean an' recharge my weapons. But I will not leave you to your own devices for any longer than need be." He stepped away from the tree. "By the time the sun's well up i' the sky, I daresay we'll once more be on our way!"

The day was indeed growing lighter. Becky could see Tyrone's shadowed form as he started across the clearing. He stopped there for a moment and turned back.

"We'll not press ahead so hard as we have done formerly. P'rhaps we'll even tarry a bit later on an' build a fire to warm an' dry ourselves. There is no longer so much chance that we might be interrupted."

The cheerful lilt in his voice made the grin that lay behind it almost visible. "I do not believe even the great MacKenzie could follow a trail that now has been washed clean o' every track an' trace o' our passin' by the night's fortuitous deluge!"

Becky had a sudden sinking feeling. She finally understood the cause of her abductor's jaunty mood. The effect of the storm on their backtrail had not before occurred to her. But now she could see clearly that what Tyrone had said was the truth. How would her father ever find them in this endless untracked wilderness with no signs to show the way?

As the day grew brighter, she watched from across the clearing while Tyrone rummaged through the leaves and scrubby undergrowth for his abandoned pack and weapons. When he'd recovered them, he took a seat on a fallen log and went about drying his rapier with a corner of his cloak. He spent several minutes afterward rubbing its blade with a piece of suet he'd taken from the pack.

Once he'd completed this task, he carefully removed the charge from his flintlock pistol and wiped that weapon clean as well. Then he reloaded it with fresh powder and ball from the horn and pouch at his side.

All of this took time, and Tyrone's attention was fully consumed by each project. He never looked in Becky's direction, knowing he'd left her with no choice but to remain in one place until he was finished with all he was doing. Only then might he trouble himself to consider her plight and return across the clearing to free her from her bonds.

Which he finally did, after what she guessed was perhaps an hour. He fetched a small oilcloth-wrapped bundle from his pack and brought it over to the magnolia where Becky remained seated on the ground. He'd taken care to leave his weapons behind on the log where he'd been working.

Without freeing her feet, he knelt behind her and untied her hands. Then he stepped back and moved around in front while unwrapping the bundle to produce a larger portion of bread than she'd so far been offered at one time. It seemed her captor was in a particularly generous mood this morning.

She accepted it without comment and began to eat. Tyrone grinned and also took from the bundle the piece of suet he'd been using to oil his blade. He held it up before her, and Becky seized it without hesitation. She stuffed it into her mouth along with the bread.

Unappetizing as it was, this was the first source of oil or protein she'd had since leaving the *Raven*. And she'd no thought of being finicky when it came to preserving her strength and energy.

When she'd finished eating, Tyrone retied her hands and went to recover his pack and weapons from the place where he'd left them. On his return he undid the rope from the tree and fastened it about her neck and shoulders as he'd done before. Then, at long last, he knelt to release the bonds from her feet.

As usual, they'd become numb during the night, and she felt sharp pricks of pain as the circulation returned. But she made no complaint as she struggled up to a standing position.

Tyrone took her in tow and led the way into the forest with a livelier stride than he'd shown on the previous day. There were still no cheery quotes from Shakespeare to spur her along in his wake. Yet, when the trees had closed around them, he did look back once to favor his prisoner with a smugly taunting grin.

Becky rewarded this with silence and a stoic expression. She simply put one foot before the other and plodded along behind, unwilling to give her captor even the slightest satisfaction from her present helpless state.

And yet, as the sky grew brighter and the sun shone down through the forest cover, she found herself starting to feel almost cheerful herself.

For one thing, the new day was showing promise of being a mild and pleasant one. A playful breeze rustled the leaves overhead, and the air was not so bitterly cold as it had been in the weeks just past. The sky she caught glimpses of through the trees was a brilliant blue with scarcely a cloud in sight.

This gave her reason to believe that last night's storm had brought with it an unseasonable but very welcome warming trend.

To add to that, she'd once again been able to leave behind a small token of her presence at their evening stopping place. This time it was a corner torn by long and patient effort from the tail of her oversized man's shirt, accomplished while her captor was busy attending to his weapons.

She'd had to leave it lying on the ground, having no way of attaching it to the smooth bole of the magnolia. But she'd found a few stones to weigh it down before covering it with her foot to keep Tyrone from seeing it. And these were arranged like a crude arrow, pointing in the direction they now were headed.

There was every reason to hope that her father's watchful eyes might come upon it if he searched the ground near that place.

26

Morning dawned clear and bright on the Gulf, with the storm-driven rollers finally starting to abate. Kirkland ordered more sail laid on and then had the taffrail log thrown out while he took sightings to estimate their current location.

There was no way to be sure, but he was very much afraid they'd made little progress westward since the previous day. And he found that the winds had pushed them farther north than he'd earlier intended, though the lookouts reported the coastal shallows of the Florida Panhandle remained below the horizon.

As for the *Raven* and her men, they'd sustained remarkably little damage as a result of the storm. Everyone had survived, and what few injuries any of them suffered were minor. The same was true of the schooner and her rigging. There was nothing that couldn't be put right in a few hours by her small but seasoned crew.

All in all, they had come out of the tempest in better condition than Kirkland had any reason to hope or expect. And for that he was grateful. But he still couldn't help begrudging the delay it had cost them. It might now be as long as two days more before they could drop anchor in the harbor at Pensacola.

With the arrival of daylight, a fresh breeze had come up from the southeast, and they were soon taking full advantage of it. But after the trials of the storm and the sleepless night, the men on the *Raven* were close to exhaustion. Kirkland ordered half of them below to get a few hours' rest while he and the remainder kept the ship on course. At midday they would do turnabout, and then he might finally have a chance to stretch out in his own bunk.

He'd no real expectation of sleeping beyond a brief catnap or two. His mind was still plagued with thoughts and concerns about the future. Some of these involved the welfare of his ship in the days ahead; others had to do with his expected meeting with the Spanish in Pensacola. He knew it might be no easy task to convince them of the seriousness of the British threat, as well as the danger of a native uprising.

And beneath all those immediate causes for worry lay the constant nagging memories of the young woman he feared he had abandoned to her fate and the malign attentions of James Tyrone. He knew, and had reminded himself more than once, that it was pointless for any commander to waste time or energy second-guessing the decisions he'd made. And he was still convinced in his mind that there had been no alternative under the circumstances.

But the mind and the heart are two different things. And nothing he could think or say to himself would ease the tightness in his chest and the lump in his throat that had been his daily companions ever since they left that anchorage on the Apalachicola.

Of course, MacKenzie—and O'Shaughnessy, as it turned out—had gone into the wilderness after them. He hoped and prayed they might meet with success. But neither of the two was a young man. And who could guess what dangers might lie in wait for them in that unforgiving country he'd heard so many stories about.

The long morning continued fair and bright, with the wind at their backs unchanging and strong. Once the storm swells had played themselves out, the Gulf became a glassy expanse of deep blue-green, with silver ripples playing about its surface. The effect was almost hypnotic. There were times when Kirkland caught himself nodding at the wheel.

At long last he was relieved by the noon watch and gladly yielded the helm to retire to the cooler darkness of his private cabin. He lay wearily down on the top of his bunk, not taking the trouble to remove his clothes or even to pull off his boots.

And in spite of what he'd thought to himself earlier, it was only a matter of a very few minutes before his eyes closed and he fell into a deep and mindless sleep of exhaustion.

Becky's notion of the "untracked wilderness" she and her captor had been traveling through was not entirely accurate. The Indians had traversed this country for thousands of years before the white man ever set foot in it. And the routes they followed by custom and habit were always those that would conduct them from one place to another with a minimum of delay or difficulty.

MacKenzie realized that while Tyrone might know nothing of this, there was little doubt that he would also try to choose for himself the path of least resistance on his way to Pensacola. It could provide them with a starting point as they set out to resume their pursuit.

For his own part, he was aware that he possessed the kind of hunter's instinct that allowed him to put himself into the mind of his quarry, be it animal or human, and so predict with a certain degree of accuracy the choices it might make. It was a skill he'd developed over long years in the wilderness, though one he'd have been hard put to explain.

Even so, the challenge that now faced his companion and himself in this new phase of their quest remained a daunting one. And he was forced to admit that any hopes for future success could very well owe more to chance than to skill or knowledge.

But all such unwanted doubts were worse than useless. He put them aside with icy resolve. All that mattered was that his only daughter was in danger. And he meant to push ahead with whatever experience and ability he could muster. And to trust these would be sufficient to accomplish her rescue.

He left their shelter in the first gray light of dawn, making his way back to the place where he had last seen signs of Tyrone and Rebecca's passing. He stood motionless in that spot for what seemed to O'Shaughnessy, who had followed, a very long time. The Irishman merely waited and watched in silence, unable to hazard even a guess as to what his companion was thinking.

What MacKenzie was doing was slowly and methodically allowing his eyes to roam over every feature of the surrounding woodland, identifying and cataloging every possible route within it. He was striving to see the place as Tyrone would have seen it, with his predictable desire to move as rapidly as possible while still keeping control of the trussed-up prisoner behind him.

At last he reached a decision. He gave his companion a brief glance and a nod. Then he started purposefully off through the trees.

O'Shaughnessy hurried to keep up. After a short distance, they came to a place where they could walk side by side. "Have y' discovered after all some trace o' their passin'?" He asked curiously. "Left behind despite the ravages o' the deluge?"

MacKenzie kept his eyes on the forest before them and did not slow his pace. "I have not," he said curtly. "'T is but a guess an' a hope that guide us now. Together wi' some wee knowledge o' the man we are after an' what I'm thinkin' is his destination."

O'Shaughnessy frowned and fell silent, choosing to save his breath for the miles ahead. What more could he ask or say after such a frank admission? He merely plodded along next to the frontiersman and kept any more questions to himself.

27

John Robert and Jeremiah had weathered the wind and the torrential downpour in the partial shelter of a grove of hardwoods, not having taken time to erect the kind of protection from the elements their father had made. They'd been in the saddle almost constantly until there was no longer enough light to see. By then they were so stiff and tired that all they'd done was drag the saddles off and tether their mounts between a couple of trees before throwing themselves down on the leaf-covered earth and going to sleep.

At least they'd had their ponchos and wide-brimmed hats to ward off the worst of the rain. And they could huddle between the four horses for warmth as well as for protection against the wind.

Beyond that there was little else they could do until the short-lived tempest played itself out and the sky began to lighten. Once the thunder had passed away to the north, they talked between themselves about the task that lay ahead. The storm's likely effect on finding the trails of their father and sister was not lost upon them. But they'd no thought to waste on that at the moment. Each thing in its own time. First they had to locate the place where the schooner had lain at anchor, somewhere north of there along the Apalachicola.

It had remained in that spot for several days apparently. And there'd been a meeting with the Indians that the sailors were still recalling and discussing among themselves. It gave the brothers reason to hope that such a large number of people moving about the area would have left signs that even the rain and the wind could not entirely erase.

When the new day finally made its appearance, they saddled up and started out again, still pushing their mounts relentlessly with the rising sun on their right and the dripping forest all around them.

They knew nearly as much about Indian trails as their father did. And one of the things they knew was that whenever possible the natives always preferred to travel the higher ground. Realizing they were within the home territory of the Creeks, they'd been keeping a watchful eye out not only for trails but also for those who might use them.

So that afternoon, when the country they rode through had grown steeper and more rugged, it was no surprise at all to come across a well-traveled path along the crests that led from south to north. Following this route north would only lead deeper into Creek lands and heighten the risk of encountering what could possibly be a hostile response. Yet the sailors Jeremiah had overheard talking were full of comments about their brief overnight stay with the natives and the daylong treks to and from their village. This path could well be the very one they had taken.

If so, there must have been a way to reach it from some place along the river. And that meant there would be another trail leading up from the water.

It took them several hours of searching to find it. But when they did, they had a pretty good notion they'd come upon the right one. Even torrential rains couldn't wash away all the clues left behind by a half dozen white men unaccustomed to the wilderness. There were scuff marks from boots on some of the rocks and broken branches that had probably been seized as handholds. There was even a soggy lump of used chewing tobacco that someone had pressed into the notch between two branches of an elm tree.

All the same, and just to be sure, Jeremiah dismounted and made his way down the steep incline to take a further look around. There was no hope of negotiating such a trail on horseback, and with Indians around someone needed to stay up above and keep an eye on their mounts. John Robert was elected for this task without discussion. Both were able trackers, but there was no question in either's mind that Jeremiah was the better.

While his brother disappeared down the forested slope, John Robert stood for several long minutes studying what he could see of the river below and of the land on either side of it. Then he picketed the horses and loosened their cinches before settling down on the grass nearby.

He sat there for a time with his arms around his knees. But as the sun grew lower in the sky, he decided Jeremiah wasn't about to return right away. He was going to take his own sweet time looking over the area for any sign and trying to work out its meaning.

So after a while he stretched out on his back and pulled his hat over his eyes.

"Well, sleepin' beauty! Reckon it wasn't a lot of use leavin' you up here on sentry duty. Couple li'l Injun girls could of prob'ly made off with all-a them horses whilst you was snoozin' the day away."

John Robert reached to push his hat back and squinted up at his brother. "Horses would of let me know all about it. Assumin' I was sleepin' so sound I couldn't hear 'em my own self. And you know that ain't too likely."

Jeremiah grinned. He knew his brother was speaking the truth. He'd just wanted to rag him a little bit. He hunkered down close by.

"Well, I got me some news," he said. "Notions, anyhow. From what-all I could see an' figure out down yonder."

"Uh-huh." John Robert sat up while Jeremiah continued.

"There was a passel of folks 'round here, one time an' another. 'Pears they had 'em some kind of a powwow in a li'l clearin' amongst the trees. Maybe a couple dozen Injuns an' some white men from the schooner. Then come night the Injuns made camp, an' next day the white folks came back. Then the whole bunch set off along this here trail."

"Pretty much the way we figured it, from what-all you told me those sailors were sayin'."

"Yep. An' a day or so later the men from the schooner came back without any of the Injuns along."

"Pa was with 'em?"

"Far as I could tell. Must not of been 'til they got back on the boat that they learned this Tyrone feller'd left an' took Becky off with him somewheres."

"You see any sign the two of 'em came this way?"

"Nope. Can't be for certain-sure with all the roustin' about here the others of 'em did. But why'd he take a chance on runnin' into that party from the boat if he lit out before they got back?"

"Or comin' up on a bunch of Injuns. Must of known they were all over this side the river a couple days earlier."

Jeremiah nodded. Then he frowned in thought. "You know, now I think on it, I seem to recall one of those sailors said he heard somebody mention Pa thought they'd be headed for Pensacola."

"Well, why'n't you say so right off?" John Robert slapped his knee. "That's good enough for me! 'Least it tells us what direction Pa'd be goin'. An' I don't reckon he's been wrong in his hunches too very often in his life!"

Jeremiah made a wry face and shrugged. "I s'pose it just kind of slipped my mind is all, what with the ridin' an' the storm an' such. But now we know it, an' the thing we got to do next is cross over to the far side of this here river."

"Uh-huh. Without wastin' 'round anymore, either. Never can tell when it may start in to flood, 'specially with all the rain we just had. You saw that driftwood lyin' high up on the bank?"

"I did. But then how an' where do we go about doin' it? This ain't exactly horse country hereabouts. And I'm not much of a mind to leave the critters behind."

"Well, li'l brother, in between all that time I was 'snoozin' the day away' I managed to study on it a mite. Seems to me I spotted a place some quarter mile to the south of here where I believe we could get these animals down to the water. An' after we've swum 'em across, that bank over yonder ain't nearly so steep an' rocky as it is on this side."

It took them less than an hour to remount and find their way down to the place John Robert was speaking of. The horses took to the dark water willingly, and as he'd once observed, all four were strong swimmers. The current was not so swift right there as to cause any serious problems, though it did carry them downstream for another short distance.

By the time they emerged dripping on the sandy, rock-strewn western shore, the sun was slipping below the trees, and it was time to look for a place to stop for the night. The horses needed rest after their long swim, and all of them could do with a warm fire that would help speed the process of drying off.

They started north toward where they assumed their father and the others would have left the river. But well before reaching that place they spotted a low, wooded hillock on their left with enough space at its top to provide a camping place surrounded by trees for concealment from possible watchers. They reined their mounts up the small rise and dismounted.

While Jeremiah unsaddled the horses and rubbed them down with some Spanish moss pulled from nearby limbs, John Robert bent more branches over and made a shelter the way his father had.

He made a small mound of tinder from his pack and dry bark from the undersides of logs; then he unloaded his pistol and struck sparks with the flint of its lock. By carefully blowing on the result, he soon had a small blaze going, its smoke dissipated by the leaves above his head.

This was to be the first real camp the brothers had had since the day they'd sighted the schooner, and they meant to take advantage of the opportunity to cook a meal for themselves and have a good night's rest. They boiled coffee and made a broth from dried beef and a few wild onions they'd saved from earlier stops along the way from St. Augustine.

The hot meal, scanty as it was, warmed and cheered them. Their supply of food was getting low. But they had no wish to take time for hunting so long as it could possibly be avoided.

They had begun to feel closer to their father and sister now than at any time since beginning their journey. Part of it was illusion perhaps, for they still had no idea how they'd manage to come upon the trail of either in the days that lay ahead.

But at least they'd made it this far, with some general idea of where the two were headed. Tomorrow would bring a new day and a fresh start to their quest.

28

High above the deck of the *Raven* the lookout in the top suddenly gave a loud cry.

"Sail ho!"

Lieutenant Kirkland woke instantly and shifted his body to swing his legs over. He sat on the edge of the bunk for a moment to shake off the drugging effects of sleep. Then he was on his feet and reaching for the cabin's door.

"Where away?!" he heard the helmsman shout as he emerged on the deck.

"Four points on the larboard quarter!"

Kirkland made his way to the mast directly under the lookout. "What nationality?" he called up to him.

"No flag showin', sir! She's a brigantine! Could be Spanish. Or . . ."

"Or British," Kirkland muttered under his breath. It was also possible, though not very likely, she was a pirate. Not many of those had the men or the wherewithal to sail such a large vessel. At any rate, she was a warship, whatever her loyalties. And that meant she could pose a serious problem for his own ship and crew.

The fact she wasn't flying any national ensign at the moment meant nothing one way or the other. Even when such a flag appeared, no wise captain would risk his ship's safety by relying on it. Showing false colors was a standard tactic among navies of the day. Only when two vessels had come within cannon shot was it customary to "show one's true colors."

"Lay on more canvas!" Kirkland cried as the rest of his crew came scrambling up on deck. "Whoever she is, we don't want any encounters with other ships out here in the open Gulf!"

The men leapt to the rigging while he went aft to take the helm. In minutes every sail the *Raven* would carry was being shaken out. The sleek schooner responded briskly, the water hissing past her bow to leave white-capped furrows in her wake.

Kirkland held to a westward course, still having no wish to chance the shoals and shallows of the Florida coast. He called up frequently to the lookout for fresh reports of the unknown vessel's bearing and location.

Before long these revealed that the brigantine's captain had decided to give chase. She'd laid on more canvas and taken a course that would intercept the *Raven*'s at some point farther ahead. With a following wind to drive her big square sails, she might be able to match or even exceed the best speed the schooner could make. With the added advantage of a closing angle, it would be only a matter of time before she closed the distance between them.

From where he stood at the wheel, Kirkland watched while Sergeant Jaynes made his way forward to load the schooner's single six-pounder cannon. An exercise in futility, he thought. The brigantine would carry at least a dozen guns, each one far heavier than the *Raven*'s own puny armament.

If Jaynes had given any consideration to this problem, his calm, practiced manner revealed no sign of it. When he'd completed the task, he came aft and wordlessly went about readying the swivel-mounted signal gun at the stern.

Then he disappeared below and reappeared several minutes later laden down with a half dozen muskets he'd taken out of the weapons locker. He seated himself on a hatch cover amidships and took his time carefully loading and priming each of them in turn.

There was no need for him to hurry. Even though the brigantine had been no more than three or four leagues behind when she started her pursuit and from the latest reports of the lookout was indeed shortening that distance, it would be hours yet before she came near enough to threaten the schooner.

Those hours dragged on with agonizing slowness. Despite the wind in their faces and the churning bow wave that left furrows in their wake, the chase gave the sense of proceeding at a snail's pace. There was only gradual change over time in the appearance of the distant vessel. And the blue-green waters of the Gulf remained flat and featureless in every direction.

Kirkland glanced at the afternoon sun from time to time, trying to estimate how much daylight was left before they might finally seize the opportunity to escape in darkness.

And meanwhile, inexorably, the brigantine crept closer.

By the time the sun was near the horizon and its golden rays began to spread fanlike over the glassy waters before them, Kirkland knew it would not disappear soon enough for his slim hope of escape by night. It was clear now that if neither vessel altered its course, the brigantine would come within cannon range before another hour had passed.

He called out commands to his crew and swung the wheel hard to starboard, willing at last to risk the unknown shoals and shallows of the Florida coast. Better that than to be trapped in the open and hopelessly outgunned by what he'd concluded long before was a hostile vessel. He knew the *Raven* would draw less water than the brigantine and hoped against hope that in whatever small respite might be bought by this latest maneuver, he could come upon some shallow cove or inlet where the heavier warship couldn't follow.

· No sooner had they made the change than the brigantine hoisted the British Union Jack and followed it up with a shot from her bow chaser as a signal that the schooner should heave to. The range was still far too great for the ball to have any effect. It splashed well astern and was cheerfully ignored by Kirkland and his men.

The brigantine's subsequent change of course was slower and clumsier than that of the nimble *Raven*. But there was no doubt that the British would keep coming. They'd follow and close the distance between them until . . .

No one gave any thought to that. They manned the sheets and held a course to the north-northwest, staying for the present beyond reach of the enemy's guns.

And every man's eyes were focused on the northern horizon, hoping for signs of approaching land.

29

For once James Tyrone had been a man of his word. It was not yet mid-morning when he called a halt and went about building a fire in the middle of a clearing surrounded by tall pines. He shed his outer garments and hung them to dry on some low-growing bushes not far from the flames. And he eased Becky's bonds so she could do the same.

If she wished. Which she didn't.

Tyrone didn't insist. His kindly attitude toward her seemed to continue—at least for the present.

He'd left her feet unbound but had fashioned one end of her "leash" into a noose that was looped more closely around her neck than it had been while they walked. He kept the other end in his hand, ready to give the rope a hard pull if she showed any sign of contentiousness. His newfound benevolence clearly had its limits.

He also maintained his customary distance from her as he dragged a log over by the fire and sat with his pistol and rapier across his knees.

Except for the noose, which she couldn't ignore, Becky paid little attention to anything the man with her in the clearing did. She seated herself on the ground near the fire and gazed into its dancing flames, studiously avoiding her captor's looks. Nor did she waste any words upon him, of either thanks or complaint.

She actually enjoyed the fire. Its cheerful warmth felt good combined with the milder weather.

After an hour or so, Tyrone rose to his feet and went to recover his clothes. He got dressed and then took up his pack, rummaging around in it with his fingers for a minute or two before removing some crusts of bread. He came and divided these more or less equally with his captive.

He also had in his hand a single slice of roast beef that he'd found in the pack. He held it up and looked across it at Becky, seeming to consider whether to share this as well. But then he shrugged and thrust it between his grinning lips.

"That, my dear," he said with his mouth full, "is the last o' the rations I brought from off the *Raven*. I fear that for the remainder o' our journey there may be naught to sustain us but some native roots an' herbs." He chewed and swallowed while eying her thoughtfully.

"Knowin' your sire as I do," he continued, "it seems probable to me that he will have imparted knowledge o' such things to his offspring. So from this time forward I'll award you the task o' findin' provender at each o' our halts."

Becky looked at him and almost smiled as certain thoughts came to her mind. But these turned out to be short lived.

"And o' tastin' every morsel o' it first, o' course." His grin grew maddeningly wider. "Before sharin' the least part wi' me!"

It took only a very few minutes to retie her hands and make preparations to resume their travels. Tyrone's actions had grown surer and more facile with practice. This time he chose to leave the noose about her neck, either from laziness or due to some streak of residual cruelty.

Becky remained silent and followed docilely behind. Her captor's more leisurely pace rendered the noose less galling than it might have been earlier.

She'd had no opportunity to leave in this spot any marks of their passing. Tyrone had kept his eyes on her almost constantly for the entire time. But there'd been no real need for it, either. Before they left, he had made only a halfhearted effort to stamp out what remained of their fire, leaving evidence in the clearing that even a child could not miss.

O'Shaughnessy's continued silence seemed to suit MacKenzie during the morning's march. He'd spoken hardly a word himself and, except for occasional brief halts to consider their surroundings, had forged ahead grimly without hesitation. If he'd doubts or reservations about the route they were now taking, he kept them strictly to himself.

The Irishman could do nothing but follow his lead, having no way to guess what mental processes led the frontiersman to choose one path over another through this apparently trackless wilderness. He could only trust his companion knew what he was about, which he certainly gave every impression of doing.

The weather, as Becky predicted from her own observations, had begun to grow noticeably warmer. This change was most evident when they left the deep forest shade to cross one of the periodic savannas under the direct rays of the sun.

After one trek of several miles over such brown, barren hills, the two men were perspiring freely under their leather and woolen clothing. And both were ready for a rest.

At last they entered the darker coolness of another broad expanse of pine forest. They proceeded for only a short distance farther until they came to a clearing among the trees. Here MacKenzie paused and looked around them for a minute or two. Then he nodded wearily and called a halt.

O'Shaughnessy offered no argument. He found a seat on a fallen log and took off his cloak to lay it across his knees.

MacKenzie sat on another log a short distance away. For a time neither of them spoke, each being a little shorter of breath than pride would let him admit. Despite MacKenzie's earlier resolve to pace himself more sensibly, the urgency of their present dilemma had tended to make him forget.

He removed his water bottle and drank deeply from it. Then he took a strip of jerky from his pack and started to chew while letting his eyes roam about the clearing. When his glance fell upon his companion, he saw that O'Shaughnessy had quenched his own thirst but afterward had taken no food.

"Y' best eat somethin' while y've the chance, man. Each o' us must keep up his strength against whatever may lie i' the future."

O'Shaughnessy simply looked at him and didn't respond.

MacKenzie got a hard biscuit and another strip of beef from his pack. "Addin' to the nourishment," he said as he started on these, "the chewin' serves to make the saliva flow an' helps to slake the thirst."

O'Shaughnessy shrugged and turned to reach into his own pack. He took out a few items of food.

Both men ate in silence for several minutes. At last MacKenzie took another drink and then rose from his place on the log to start walking slowly about the clearing with his eyes on the ground.

O'Shaughnessy simply sat where he was and watched, pleased to enjoy a few added minutes of rest before having to set out once more on their seemingly endless quest.

He saw his companion pause for a moment beside a large magnolia tree at one side of the clearing, then suddenly kneel to look closely at something under its overhanging branches.

"Aha!" he exclaimed. "She has done it again!"

"She?" O'Shaughnessy leaned forward but could see nothing from his place on the log. "Your daughter, d' you mean?"

"Aye. Another bit o' cloth, an' she's left upon it this time a gather o' stones to point us the way!"

O'Shaughnessy's curiosity got the better of his weariness. He stood and crossed to where MacKenzie was kneeling and peered down over his shoulder.

"A corner o' that shirt she was wearin', begorra! An' no mistakin' about it!"

"Aye. Wi' these pebbles here i' the shape of an arrow!"

MacKenzie sat back on his heels; his shoulders sagged with relief. "'T was only a series o' thoughtful guesses that brought us to this place. An' I will confess to y' now, I was havin' some doubts i' my mind whether those guesses might lead us astray." He smiled up at his companion. "But thanks to a bit o' luck an' aid from the Almighty, those doubts are now behind us. From this place on we may begin to seek further such signs left behind by my clever daughter!"

They hurried to retrieve their packs and weapons, then set out in the direction the pebbles were pointing. Even O'Shaughnessy felt a renewed sense of hope and vigor as he strode along beside his companion.

And neither had any hint as yet of the overconfident vanity of Dread Jamie Tyrone, who had begun to slow his journey with no thought that he still might be followed.

30

The coast of the Florida Panhandle had finally come into sight. Beyond a narrow expanse of long, low beaches, a wide green band of forest could be made out. At places the beaches were overtaken by dark masses of twisted hardwoods stretching almost down to the water.

But as the *Raven* swung west to follow the shore, there was no sign of any break in these features to suggest some sheltering inlet or river. The men aboard her had little choice but to continue on in hopes of finding such a refuge before the brigantine could approach within cannon shot.

The British ship had lost headway when the schooner altered her course, but it did not take her long to start making up the distance. With a strong and steady following wind, the respite gained by Kirkland and his crew could be no more than another brief hour or two.

The sun in their faces was touching the sea now. Yet the blue canopy of the sky remained free of clouds, and darkness still lay sometime in the future. There would be more than enough daylight left for the brigantine to close and bring the *Raven* under her guns unless some means of escape was found quickly.

The pursuing vessel was holding somewhat farther out to sea than the schooner, no doubt wary of shoals and hidden reefs. But once she had managed to come abreast, this would just put her in a better position for a broadside.

The northern sky was slowly turning a dark gray-blue. Too slowly! Kirkland had to force himself to resist calling up to the lookout for frequent reports of what could be seen to landward. The man knew every bit as well as he did how desperate the situation was. And he'd been assigned that post earlier because he was known to have the sharpest eyes of anyone in the crew.

The others kept glancing back over the stern to where the sails of the British ship kept looming larger, fully visible now without the aid of greater height. Reports of her approach came unbidden to Kirkland at the helm, more often and more stridently than he would have liked.

After what seemed an eternity, there came a cry from above: "White water broad on the starboard bow! Open water beyond! Looks to be a pass into some big bay or other!"

"Leeway to make a crossing?" Kirkland asked with a shout.

"Green water maybe a cable length wide! Can't speak for the depth!"

"Broad on the starboard bow" meant they were almost abreast of the opening before it was spotted. There was no time to worry about draft or anything else. This was likely the only chance they had.

Kirkland swung the wheel hard over while his crew, who'd been standing ready at the booms and sheets, redirected the sails.

These flapped and luffed as they made the sudden turn. But the *Raven* swiftly regained headway and made straight for the opening between whitecaps while under full sail.

They were taking a desperate chance; yet none had any doubts that the danger behind them was greater. Kirkland set his jaw and gripped the wheel tightly, steering a course through the pass and into the smooth expanse of water beyond.

They made it with room to spare—and with no scraping of the schooner's bottom over shallows or shoals. The instant they were across, Kirkland called for sail to be taken in. Then he breathed a long sigh of relief and set himself to surveying their latest surroundings.

Behind them in the Gulf the crew and captain of the brigantine had been caught completely by surprise. Their furious shouts and orders could be heard echoing across the water as sailors scrambled to the rigging and sought to alter their course.

It was a slow and clumsy business. The fore-and-aft rigged mizzen came about readily enough. But the big square sails of the mainmast could be redirected only by twisting the yards. And with a full complement of canvas billowing from every one, the British ship lost weigh and seemed to flounder in the water.

A cheer went up from the men on the schooner when they saw this result. But Kirkland raised his voice to quell the jubilation and bring everyone back to the matters at hand.

"Finish taking in sail and keep a sharp eye out for shallows! We're in unknown waters here, and if we happen to run aground, the Brits may come inside and seize the lot of us at their leisure!"

After their progress had slowed, Kirkland pointed their bow to the east where their hull was hidden from the Gulf behind a low headland. Their masts would still be visible above it for a time. But the lookout reported that the British didn't seem inclined to continue their pursuit for now. They'd finally managed to bring their ship around and were sailing parallel to the shore.

No doubt a sensible captain would want to take soundings before trying the pass. And with darkness near he'd likely wait until tomorrow. If he chose to enter the bay at all.

He might just sail off and go on about his business. But it would be foolish to risk the *Raven* on such a possibility. There had been ample depth in the pass for themselves and could be for the brigantine as well. Especially when the tide was high.

Which meant they still had to find some refuge where they could be out of sight by day and in water too shallow for the larger ship to follow—a tree-shrouded cove, perhaps, or a river that emptied into this bay. Kirkland knew there were many such hiding places everywhere on the Florida coast. Their problem at the moment was finding one in the short time remaining before darkness closed in.

There was another problem that would confront them in the future. Their recent move to escape had just put them in a bottle. Whether the British negotiated the pass into the bay or remained outside it keeping watch, either would deny their return to the Gulf and hopes of reaching Pensacola.

None of this had been lost on Kirkland. But one problem at a time. He'd cross that bridge when he came to it.

They sailed east for a short distance, but then the lookout reported a great expanse of reed-choked shallows ahead. It extended out into the bay for more than a mile and would make any approach to land in that direction impossible.

Kirkland swallowed his frustration and ordered the schooner brought about. They headed for the northern shore, which was farther away. Its features were dark and hazy in the fading light.

When they neared the opposite shore, they found it was high and hilly, with no obvious breaks in its lines to suggest the presence of inlets or streams. It angled from northeast to southwest, and they followed it for a mile or so until it made a sharp turn back to the north. Here the sailors at the rail called out that there appeared to be a current, which could be the outflow of a river.

A little farther on, this proved to be the case. And not a moment too soon! By now it was so dark that the entrance was only a wide black avenue between the blacker shapes of trees that loomed on each side.

Kirkland ordered a man to the bow with a sounding line and took the risk of posting another there with a lantern to light the way. The others took up pikes to fend off snags or shoals while they cautiously advanced upstream.

There turned out to be little need for the last. The river continued wide and deep until it curved around a high bluff that was tall enough to conceal them from any watchers on the bay.

Kirkland looked up at this and decided they'd come far enough for tonight. He brought the *Raven* alongside the bank and had her tied up to some trees while the last of the sails were taken in.

If the British were to enter this river by day, the schooner's presence could be clearly seen. But first they'd have to cross the broad water of the bay. And by then he meant to have taken better stock of their surroundings with a thought to moving her to a safer location.

In anticipation of this change, he ordered two men to keep watch. One would remain on the schooner and the other would go ashore and climb to the top of the bluff that overlooked the bay. Each would be relieved at midnight and again at dawn.

Short-handed as they were, that was the most he could do. He had a meal prepared for the crew of salt pork and hardtack. Then those who weren't on watch retired for the night.

He spent little time in his cabin fretting over the future. There was no way he could guess what the next move of the British might be. Or what they themselves could do in response. With luck, the captain of the brigantine would realize the difficulty of a prolonged search and simply sail away to leave them to their own devices.

If he didn't . . .

It had been a long and trying day. After only a few minutes, Kirkland slept.

31

In addition to their prolonged break of the morning, Tyrone decided to call an early halt for the night. Part of his reason, of course, was to give Becky more time to seek food for their supper. But he also seemed in no hurry to reach the end of their journey now that he believed himself safe from pursuit. He smiled often and appeared to be enjoying the more leisurely pace he'd begun setting for them.

Becky had her own reasons for welcoming the delay.

Tyrone untied her hands but left the noose about her neck, keeping hold of the long end of the rope while giving her a chance to move more or less freely about their current surroundings. He watched with interest as she studied the area for several minutes and then knelt to pull some stalks from the prickly pear cactus that lay scattered about the floor of the forest. She held these up carefully.

"You'll need to build a fire to burn off the thorns," she said. "But you'll find the flesh nourishing and filling, if somewhat lacking in taste."

He took them gingerly and laid them aside, keeping his eyes on her while she moved about on her knees and started to sift through a pile of leaves.

"Might find a few nuts around here too," she said thoughtfully, as if to herself. "Or acorns at least." Suddenly she bent and made a swift grabbing motion with her hands. "Aha!"

She sat back to hold up a wriggling creature she'd apparently startled from its hiding place. She gave Tyrone a wry grin as she dangled it by the tail. It was a legless lizard about a foot in length, repulsive to look at but plump enough to offer a few bites of meat.

If she expected Tyrone to be put off by such an unsavory item of food, she was quickly disappointed. He came and took it from her without hesitation, severing its head with a flash of his dagger. Without taking his eyes off her, he retreated a few feet and sat on the ground to finish skinning and cleaning it. Then he spitted it on the stalk of a palmetto in preparation for the fire he'd be making.

Becky searched for a bit longer but found nothing else to eat in the range of her tether. When she suggested she might gather some cattails from a spring-fed creek a little way off, Tyrone smiled and shook his head. He reeled her in and bound her ankles, then went about making a fire with sparks from the lock of his unloaded pistol.

She watched while Tyrone took each of the prickly pears by the stem and held it in the heat until the thorns flared up and disappeared. He laid these aside one by one, then took up the spit to roast the scant flesh of the lizard.

When he'd concluded this was done, he gathered up all the items of their supper and brought them across to where Becky was sitting. He divided the meal between them, including a small strip of meat he cut off to hand his prisoner.

Then he situated himself on the ground a few yards away and watched intently while she ate. He tasted nothing himself for several long minutes, paying special attention after she'd chewed the lizard's flesh and swallowed it. Evidently he'd heard or suspected that some reptiles contained poisons harmful to humans and other animals.

After they'd both finished eating, Tyrone retied Becky's hands but then lifted the noose from around her neck. He let her stay where she was and went to sit on the ground again a short distance away.

For a minute or two he looked at what remained of the dying fire. Then he leaned back on his elbows and turned his head toward her. For what seemed an uncomfortably long time, he gazed at her in silence with a half smile on his lips. She avoided his eyes.

At last he spoke.

"Y' know"—his voice was mild in the evening stillness—"I do believe you are the most untalkative woman it has been my considerable experience to encounter. You have scarce said three dozen words to me in all the long days we have traveled together."

Becky didn't look at him and saw no reason to reply.

"I have not treated you so badly as I might well ha' done—considerin' the hostile nature o' your demeanor toward me. The bonds that keep you wi' me are no doubt awkward an' uncomfortable. But no more than prudent to my way o' thinkin'. I've willin'ly shared food wi' you an' let you drink"—he paused and his voice became softer—"while keepin' a rein on my deeper desires."

Becky still said nothing.

"Have you no words at all for me, then?" Tyrone persisted. "No hint o' kindness or friendly feelin'?" He noted the look on her face and shrugged. "Or p'rhaps for the present a few heartfelt curses. Anything at all to reveal a small bit o' warmth beneath that arctic exterior."

Becky glanced at him and looked away again. "What is it you think I should say?" she responded in a flat, indifferent voice.

"That, o' course, must be up to you. For myself, anythin' else but continued silence will be heartily welcome."

"And why is that? Have you grown tired of your own taunting words? You want me to whimper and beg now to exult in my misery?"

Tyrone, still lying back on his elbows, shook his head. "It is not that, lass. It is only that if we are to spend the rest o' our lives together, there must be some sort o' commerce between us."

Becky turned at last and stared at her captor with wide, fearful eyes. The rest of their lives! Such a possibility had not entered her mind. Death, perhaps. With luck instead, a long-awaited rescue. But years and years spent in bondage to this man! There were no words to describe such a nightmare.

After a moment, Tyrone sat up and smiled. "Surely you must ha' garnered some slight inklin' o' my intentions. From the very first meetin' in my cabin I framed my resolve. That, I said to myself, is a woman! Strong-willed an' a bit o' a harridan, to be sure. But wi' a fine youth an' beauty for all o' it. Just the sort o' wife to brighten the declinin' years o' old Jamie Tyrone!"

Becky realized her mouth was hanging open, and she closed it with a snap.

"I've a goodly fortune put by," the man beside her went on, "amassed from my various enterprises here an' abroad. An' wi' a bit o' consideration for what I can relate to our English friends in Pensacola, we'll be able to depart that primitive backwater in comfort."

Tyrone's smile grew broader as he spoke about the future. "First we'll find a willin' priest among the dons so that all will be respectable an' proper. Then we'll board ship for the auld country—Kinsale, p'rhaps, or even Dublin-town. I'll purchase an estate in the country, an' we'll live out our days there in the style o' the landed gentry!"

Becky's astonishment turned into fury at the sheer unvarnished arrogance of the man. He had her entire future planned with no thought for herself or her wishes! She was on the verge of unleashing her rage upon him when she hesitated, seeing the futility of such an outburst. It might anger him and lead to greater brutality, or—perhaps worse—it would merely be ignored.

Neither would help her escape that ominous future. She expected a "willin' priest" could be found who'd overlook any reluctance on the part of a mere woman once silver crossed his palm. And afterward? Wife beating was hardly unknown even among the most respectable "country squires."

She took a deep breath and gritted her teeth. Tyrone's overweening vanity, so fully displayed just now, might turn out to be her best hope. At least it was worth a try.

Becky lowered her eyes and did her best to give the impression of a shy maiden who'd been momentarily overwhelmed. "This is all," she said softly, "so unexpected." She paused and glanced up at him under lashes that fluttered ever so slightly. "You must give me a little time to consider it."

"Consider by all means!" Tyrone said expansively. "Consider to your heart's content! 'T will be a few days longer before we arrive in Pensacola. An' then we will be wed wi' no need o' further considerin'!"

A few days longer. For her father to find them. Or for her to try some desperate action of her own. There was no doubt in her mind that one or the other must occur. She would *not* be the wife of this beast of a man! That would literally be, to Becky, a fate worse than death!

Neither of them spoke for the rest of the evening. Tyrone kept his distance, though his eyes never left her until the day had faded slowly into night. Just before then, with his usual "prudence," he'd replaced the noose about her neck and secured its other end to the bole of a tree.

She slept little after darkness came, succumbing to only rare and unintentional catnaps—which always ended with her eyes jerking open to stare into the blackness with vague recollections of some terrifying dream.

She shivered then, though the weather had been much warmer during the past several days.

32

As soon as day began to brighten the streamers of mist that rose about their river anchorage, Lieutenant Kirkland went ashore to climb the bluff that overlooked the waters beyond it. He wanted to see for himself whether the British brigantine remained in the area and if she intended to enter the bay in search of the *Raven*.

He did not have long to wait. The tide from the Gulf appeared to be rising, and soon the jib and square topsails of the warship appeared in the passage. He watched through his spyglass as her men took soundings and she advanced slowly and cautiously between the shoal waters on either side. In the end, she navigated the entrance without difficulty and afterward began a careful circuit of the bay, moving in a counterclockwise direction much as the schooner had done the evening before.

Kirkland uttered a silent curse. He gave the sailor on watch his spyglass and a pistol with instructions to fire it if—and only if—the brigantine approached the mouth of the same river where the *Raven* was hiding. Then he quickly scrambled down the bluff and returned to his ship.

Every man of his crew was fully awake and alert now, ready for any orders their captain might issue. All of them were well aware of the danger they could be facing.

Kirkland had the mooring lines brought aboard, and the schooner was eased back into the slow-moving current with pikes and oars. They brought her about in midstream so that she could advance upriver with her bow pointed toward the exit into the bay. This would make a departure from the place faster and easier—if and when that turned out to be possible. It would also ensure that their cannon in the bow could be directed toward any would-be pursuers.

They crept upstream, staying close to the shore and using pikes and oars to move the schooner along. With a fuller crew, they might have towed her with a longboat. But at the present time they had too few men and no such boat.

It was an agonizingly slow process. Yet, after a couple of hours, they had made it far enough to round a curve and find a place along the bank that was partially concealed by overhanging trees. Kirkland decided this was probably the best they could do. He'd no idea how much farther the waterway might remain navigable, and he didn't want to risk running aground or making their leaving this location any slower or more difficult than it already would be.

There was nothing else to do now but wait and hope for the best. There was still a reasonable chance they wouldn't be discovered. The bay they'd entered was a large one, and surely this wasn't the only waterway or inlet where a ship of the *Raven*'s size and draft could be hidden.

If worst came to worst and the brigantine did find this river and manage to probe this far up it, there would no longer be any real choice but to abandon their ship and take to the land. Kirkland didn't expect it to happen, but if it did, they'd be in no worse—or better—shape than MacKenzie and O'Shaughnessy. But such an event would almost surely put paid to their plans to give warning to the Spaniards.

Sergeant Jaynes went about reloading and priming the cannon. Then he and the sailors did the same with the muskets. The sea air and the night's dampness had made it more than possible that the earlier loads would fail or misfire if it turned out they were needed.

Hours passed with no signal from their watchman and no other way to guess what the British might be doing. It felt oppressively still on the river. There was little breeze to stir the leaves overhead, and only the sound of cicadas and periodic cries of hunting waterfowl broke the silence to remind them that they weren't the only creatures left on earth.

By the time the sun had passed its zenith, Kirkland could stand the waiting no longer. He had the jolly boat put over the side and left Jaynes in command of the schooner while he set out downstream with a sailor to relieve the watch and with plans to see what he could of the present situation for himself.

He realized there might be a certain amount of risk involved in this action, and in some quarters it could even be considered a dereliction of duty to abandon his ship in the presence of an enemy. It would surely have been more prudent to send a couple of sailors instead. But he'd always been a man of action, and submitting to forced inactivity was just not in his nature.

When they'd reached their former anchorage and made it to the top of the bluff, the sailor who'd been left behind was more than happy to see them—

mostly, it seemed, out of boredom and lack of company instead of any threat from the British. While Kirkland took the glass and opened it to scan the bay, the watchman made his report.

"She sailed 'round an' about out yonder for some three, four hours, never comin' in too close to land. Worried 'bout shoals an' shallows, I figure. 'Peared to be takin' soundin's right regular while she did it. An' I seen the cap'n with a spyglass up on the quarter deck, lookin' everwhere he could think of to look along these shores."

The sailor paused and turned his head to spit tobacco juice. Then he shrugged.

"I reckon he never did come to no conclusions about where it was we might of gone an' holed up. 'Cause finally they just come about an' made it back towards that pass what leads out yonder into the Gulf. Crossed it somethin' like a hour ago, I guess, or maybe a little more recent."

Kirkland nodded and swung his glass toward the passage and what he could see of the waters beyond it. He scowled.

"And there she is, sure enough. Just holding on station and watching for us to make our move to come out. I wonder how long her captain is willing to play that waiting game." He paused, then added more quietly, "Or how long we can afford to stay caught in his net."

He left the sailor he'd arrived with to remain on watch, while he and the other man descended the bluff and boarded the boat to return to the schooner.

He spent the journey considering his options.

It seemed there were only two: stay hidden where they were and hope to wait the British out, or try to make a run for the open sea—which would amount to certain suicide unless it could be somehow accomplished in darkness. Neither choice held much appeal.

On the one hand, their available rations were beginning to run short and there was still an urgent need to warn the Spanish of the enemy threat. On the other, a night passage into the Gulf would be a desperate gamble that could easily end in disaster. Any helpful illumination from the moon or stars would also reveal them to the British. And without it they'd need incredible luck to keep from running aground and finding themselves at dawn a stationary target for the brigantine's guns.

As they drew near to the *Raven*'s hiding place, he recalled seeing something once on a chart that made him wonder if there might be a third possibility. It was a slim hope at best and depended on his estimate of the actual location of this unidentified bay. But he had the rest of the afternoon to study the charts he'd found aboard and decide whether his unlikely idea might be feasible.

33

Tyrone arose at first light but afterward seemed in no particular hurry to resume their journey. He took his time taking up his weapons and other belongings and wiping the dew from them with his cloak. Then he spent some more minutes stamping out and scattering the remains of their fire.

Finally he ambled across the clearing to untie Becky's ankles and release the rope that secured the noose at her neck to the tree. He favored her with a cheerful grin while he did this. But he didn't speak until he'd stepped back away from her with the longer rope in his hands.

"I believe we will forego any search for provender at present," he said, "until we come upon a more promisin' stoppin' place. There does not appear to be much else of interest to us here." His grin became broader, and he made a slight bow. "P'rhaps you will offer a suggestion when you espy some likely settin'."

Becky nodded and forced herself to smile. She did not trust herself to utter a reply. She was afraid her anger and desperation might reveal themselves in her voice. There seemed no choice for the present but to let this foolish man believe she might actually consider with favor the prospect he'd laid before her the previous evening.

They set off through the trees at an unhurried pace. After three or four hours, they came to a grassy place that sloped down to a spring-fed creek that gurgled cheerfully by, its sparkling ripples catching highlights from the sun. Here and there it turned back on itself, and in the quieter pools Becky could see stands of cattails and watercress stalks. A short distance to their right was a parklike area shaded by live oaks and other hardwoods.

It was without question a pleasing scene. But its possibilities for the immediate future were what most appealed to Tyrone's sharp-eyed captive. She took a deep breath and composed her face into the best pretense of rapture she could manage.

"Oh, what a lovely place!" she murmured softly from where she'd paused a few feet behind. "It's almost as if a kindly Providence just put it here so two people could rest and become better acquainted!"

Tyrone turned to look at her, his forehead creased in a skeptical frown. After a moment, this expression was replaced by a smile of his own. "Do y' truly think so, lass?" He turned back and viewed their surroundings as if seeing them for the first time. "Well, now that you speak of it, I do confess there is a certain charm to the spot. I suppose we might tarry here for a short while."

He paused and thought for a moment, then turned again to meet her eyes. "Do y' believe we might find somethin' to break our fast hereabout?"

"Oh, yes!" Becky's passionate response wasn't entirely feigned. But its reason wasn't quite what she wanted the man with her to think. "There are cattail roots and fresh greens over there. And we can find acorns under the trees."

She paused and let a brief frown cross her face. Then she shrugged and said slowly, "But I'm afraid the last will not be very good to eat unless we let them soak in the stream for a while to wash out the bitterness. It could take several hours."

Tyrone waved a hand expansively. "Well, go ahead an' gather 'em up along wi' the rest! I am now feelin' a great hunger come upon me. An' there's no longer a need for haste at present, so long as we'll have food an' water in plenty."

He fell silent for a moment and smiled at her warmly. "P'rhaps we may even remain in this place for the night!"

Becky returned the smile and managed to avoid shuddering under his gaze. *Perhaps*, she thought to herself, *you've less time to tarry than you may suppose, with my father close behind.* And she prayed this was true.

She stood submissively while her hands were unbound to allow her the freedom to search for food. Tyrone seemed more than willing today to let her range as far as she needed in order to supplement the collection. He simply followed a few yards behind, keeping a firm grip on the rope connected to the noose that chafed her neck.

She went first to the stream to pluck cattail roots and gather watercress. She made two trips, bringing armfuls back and piling them on the grass not too far from the grove of trees. Then she entered the woods and scrambled about on her knees for almost an hour seeking acorns, which she collected in the fold of her untucked shirt.

When she'd deposited these by the greens, she hesitated and glanced at Tyrone. He was leaning his back against the bole of a tree, watching her calmly with that maddening smile on his lips. He'd made no comments about her selection of foods and seemed to have little interest in them besides perhaps in their quantity.

So, with a mental shrug, she made another trip to the edge of the forest and plucked a number of fleshy stalks from the prickly pear cactus that was lying about nearby. She said nothing as she dropped these on the ground by the other items. But both she and her captor knew another fire would be needed to burn off the thorns and make them edible.

And this would mean a longer delay and another clear sign of their presence here. The more time it took to prepare and consume their midday meal, the greater the chance Tyrone might indeed decide to remain in this spot for the night. And the more time it would give her father to follow and finally to catch up with them. It was the single overriding obsession behind every action that Becky now took.

Tyrone made the fire willingly enough while she set about shelling the acorns. She wrapped the yellowish meat in a bundle made from a small piece of burlap and some string that had been found in her captor's pack. He followed her to the edge of the creek where she submerged the bundle in the swift-flowing water and secured the end of the string to a branch hanging over it.

Then they returned to the fire, and Becky was invited to have a seat on the cool grass under the trees so that Tyrone could bind up her ankles. The rope was not so painfully tight as she'd earlier been used to. But there was still no chance of undoing the knots with his watchful eyes constantly on her.

Tyrone went about singeing the thorns off the prickly pears; then he came and laid a portion of all the food at her side. He stretched himself out on the ground nearby, close enough for conversation but still safely outside her reach.

They spent some time in the leafy shade while they satisfied their hunger. Afterward there followed a silence between them. Tyrone picked his teeth with the nail of a finger and seemed content to simply enjoy the sounds of the stream and the stirrings of tiny creatures in the forest behind them.

His relaxed mood told Becky it was time to go farther with the plan she'd been working on since last night.

She looked over at him and spoke quietly and a bit hesitantly. "You told me only a very little about yourself yesterday. And a girl likes to know more about a man she would marry. Do you suppose perhaps today you might . . . ?"

She lowered her eyes and let her voice lapse into silence. She held her breath while Tyrone glanced at her and seemed to consider for a minute.

"'T is a fair request," he said then. "Such a tale o' adventure an' achievement ought be shared wi' a man's woman."

He situated himself more comfortably, leaning back on his elbows. And after a brief pause, the former pirate started to talk.

It took little encouragement for "Dread Jamie Tyrone" to warm to the subject of his past. It was clear he'd had some notions of own about how they might "become better acquainted" in the way she'd suggested when they arrived here. And building himself up in her eyes was an agreeable first step.

Nor was it in his nature to share any conversation equally. He talked almost constantly about himself for the best part of the afternoon.

Which suited Becky's intentions perfectly. She needed to contribute only smiles and periodic murmurs of admiration. She recalled that her sister-in-law Mary had once told her that the secret to winning any man's affection was to keep silent and let him do the talking.

He recounted at length his experiences as a "privateer" and "slave importer"—giving special emphasis to all the riches these ventures had brought him. Along the way he spiced his narrative with lively accounts of fights at sea and the duels he'd personally fought and won.

His vain self-esteem seemed matched only by his crass insensitivity.

Somehow it slipped his mind to mention his aborted scheme to seize the governorship of East Florida some twenty years earlier, as well as the accompanying loss of a small fortune in gold to Becky's then youthful father.

She, of course, knew this story at least as well as Tyrone. It had been related more than once in the MacKenzie household—most often as an illustration of the uncertainties of the world and how bold action might overcome these.

But now was not the time to mention unpleasant subjects. She wanted to let the man ramble on, painting as glowing a picture of himself as his huge conceit might lead him to. And to take every minute and hour that was needed in order to do it.

At long last he seemed to run out of more lies to tell. He paused and looked across at her as if expecting some sort of response.

Becky forced her lips into yet another admiring smile and said, with what she hoped would sound like shy fascination, "Well, as you said, you've led a very adventurous and . . . interesting . . . life. I can scarcely think of another whose experiences would compare."

Actually she could. But she kept the fact to herself.

Tyrone accepted the compliment with a self-assured chuckle. "An' so then, do you think p'rhaps y' might find life wi' such a man to your likin' goin' forward?"

"I . . . might," She responded coyly. "If only you'll permit me just a little more time to accustom my thinking to it."

She avoided his eyes and tilted her head back to look up at the late-afternoon sky. "It will be dark in another few hours," she said, changing the subject, "and I don't look forward to plodding ahead through the forest shadows. Didn't you say we might possibly spend the night here?"

"I did indeed," Tyrone agreed. "An' the prospect appeals to my weary bones as well. We'll just enjoy a long refreshin' sojourn in this place. An' we'll make a fresh start upon the morrow."

Becky hesitated a minute and then glanced at him with hooded eyes. "There is only one thing I must ask of you, though," she said shyly, "on this night of all nights. When I'm just beginning to see you in a different light." She paused again before concluding quietly, "That you not now try to take any . . . liberties . . . with me."

Tyrone didn't speak for several long minutes. She eyed him covertly and saw warring emotions on his features: anger, petulance, frustrated passion, and finally a kind of grim resolve.

"I have not done so in all these days past," he said, as if through gritted teeth, "as you very well know. So I believe I may contain my fond desire for a short time longer. Our weddin' night will be all the sweeter for the anticipation!"

Becky said nothing more while Tyrone bound her wrists and went about securing the rope with the noose to a nearby tree. Whatever "fond desire" he might claim to feel still didn't involve allowing her any greater freedom.

And as she lay quietly, waiting for the onset of darkness, an urgent voice inside her head kept repeating over and over, *Hurry, Father! Oh please, please hurry!*

Lest that anticipated wedding night became a terrible and inescapable reality!

34

John Robert and Jeremiah spent the morning searching the west bank of the Apalachicola River for sign. They found little—only a few broken branches that might have meant something had there been tracks or other marks to go with them. But of those there were none. The heavy storm had indeed washed the place "as clean an' bare as the day this world was created."

The only clue they had to go on was an overheard sailor's remark that their father and those he pursued might be headed toward Pensacola—which lay many miles to the west-southwest of their present location. And the only advantage they had was the four horses that would enable them to move more swiftly than the others could on foot.

"Well," Jeremiah said after several fruitless hours of scouring the area within a few hundred yards of the river, "this here is turnin' out to be pretty much a flat waste of time. We need to think of some other way to go about findin' where Pa an' them others went."

"I know it," John Robert agreed, frowning. "An' I've had me a notion 'bout what else we might do. But the trouble of it is, that notion's liable to cost us even more time—least in the short run."

"You reckon it's somethin' could bring us up on their trail in the long run?"

"I reckon. Sooner or later."

"Well, later's a whole heap better'n never. What's your idea?"

"Head on out from here towards the southwest, 'til we figure it's a tad further'n any of 'em would of got to when that storm hit 'em. Then start back 'round to the north an' east kind of in a half-circle, cuttin' for sign. Must be tracks out yonder left by somebody after the rain." He shrugged. "If we don't come on 'em the first go-round, then we just move on out a mite further an' circle back the other way."

"Uh-huh." Jeremiah nodded. "Ought to work. But like you say, it's goin' to take a while."

"Best I can come up with. You got any other notions?"

"Nope. I reckon we'd best be about it then." Jeremiah, who'd been searching the ground on foot, swung up into the saddle. He walked his horse to where John Robert sat his own mount holding the reins of the spare horses.

As he came alongside, John Robert had another thought. "Somethin' else we'd ought to be doin' whilst we're huntin' for tracks is keepin' our eyes out for likely campin' places. Need to get down an' study on that kind of a spot real extra careful."

"Uh-huh," Jeremiah said, lifting his reins.

Without further words they set out at a distance-eating trot, taking advantage of the open pine barren and grass-covered savanna ahead of them for as long as these might last.

They rode steadily through the afternoon and had little chance to search for signs of their father's or sister's passing. By the time they reached a point where they thought those others might have continued their trek following the storm, the day was almost done.

They found a grassy clearing among the trees, unsaddled and picketed the horses, and then shared some jerky and hard biscuits before spreading their blankets for the night. The weather was mild enough that they did not trouble to build a fire but simply stretched out on the ground with their saddles for pillows. And within a very few minutes, both were quietly asleep.

Kirkland had wasted no time after returning aboard the *Raven* in taking out his sextant and recording several careful sights on the sun. Then he dug out all the charts they had and brought them below with him into the salon. He laid these out on the deal table and seated himself to pore over them.

˒Their latitude at present was roughly equal to that of Pensacola, perhaps just a little north of the Spanish port. As for how far they were away from it, he could only make a guess. But after considering carefully their speed on the previous day and the distance he thought they'd come, he did not believe it would be more than thirty or forty miles. Add to that the features of the coast they'd passed during the late afternoon, and it seemed very possible that the low beach that had been on their left when they crossed into this bay could be the eastern tip of Santa Rosa Island.

He found the place on a chart and bent forward to study it more closely. Santa Rosa was a thirty-mile-long barrier island that protected the bay of Pensacola along its western extent. And at its other end was another broad bay that seemed to correspond with the one they had entered.

The distance between island and mainland appeared to range from less than half a mile on this side to as much as three miles in the west. What mattered most, however, was the depth of the water inside. Records of soundings on the chart suggested a vessel of the *Raven*'s shallow draft might just be able to travel its entire length.

Perhaps this was so, and perhaps it was not. Frequent storms and tides along the Florida coast made all such notations questionable at best. Kirkland frowned and thought about that for a long and agonizing time. Then he thought about the other very limited options that remained open to them.

At last he made his decision. In for a penny, in for a pound. It was a long chance to take, with a good possibility they would find themselves aground somewhere in the passage and forced to continue in a small boat or on foot to a meeting with the Spaniards.

But he doubted the brigantine would risk following at all events. Even if she could manage to negotiate the shallow waterway, the more closely she approached the Spanish outposts, the more likely she'd be to find herself under Spanish guns and facing capture in the process.

He rolled up the charts and went to explain the plan to his crew. Before long they'd freed the schooner from its moorings and started her downriver to their earlier position behind the high bluff.

There they waited with all hands in readiness for the sun to slip behind the trees.

When the shadows had grown long and the shores of the lake had begun to grow vague in haze and darkness, they recovered the lone watchman from the top of the bluff and crept cautiously around the headland with jib and topsail only.

They continued to skirt the forested fringe of the bay for some four or five miles where it curved around to the southwest. The black-painted *Raven* was almost invisible against the trees except for the small, buff shapes of slowly moving sails. The lookout reported no unusual activity aboard the British ship, which lay outside in the still sunlit Gulf.

When they came abreast of a large headland with a broad inlet beyond it, the schooner's bow was pointed directly south. Kirkland shouted an order to his waiting crew, and every sail the *Raven* would bear was instantly shaken out. Her bow lifted, and she surged forward into bright sunlight, headed for the entrance to the passage that could take them to Pensacola.

And finally the brigantine responded, swinging around to bring her broadside to bear on the ship they could see beyond the low, featureless beach that lay between them. No more warning shots this time. She meant to rake the schooner fore and aft the moment she drew in range.

And at that moment Kirkland threw the wheel hard over and made for the narrow gap between mainland and barrier island. The sudden move had been planned, and the crew responded without hesitation. The *Raven* scarcely lost headway as she swung her bow to the west.

The brigantine immediately let go her broadside. But her aim was poor, and the only damage she inflicted was a single hole in the mizzen and a topsail yard swept away; the rest of the shots splashed harmlessly. Well before the British could reload, the *Raven* had slipped behind a higher dune and started taking in sail to negotiate the narrow passage.

Even if he wished to follow, the brigantine's captain had placed himself in an impossible position to do it soon. He'd been sailing west when the schooner made her sudden appearance and would have to come about to enter the pass into the bay—a time-consuming maneuver for the large, square-rigged vessel.

Instead, he held course to the west for a time, staying safely beyond the coastal shallows. The dunes and the distance made another broadside hardly worth the trouble.

When the sun was almost touching the Gulf, the *Raven*'s lookout reported the British vessel had finally given up the pursuit. Her sails grew smaller and more distant, then finally sank below the horizon.

35

MacKenzie and O'Shaughnessy had camped late and risen early to resume their trek through the hills of West Florida. They had spent a long and wearying day in pursuit of Tyrone and his prisoner. But their resolve had been bolstered by the certain knowledge that they were once again on the right trail.

There were tracks now in the soft ground that had been left after the rain. And they'd discovered the remains of a fire some half dozen miles beyond the place where they'd found Becky's message for them under the magnolia. It had been larger than anything an Indian or frontiersman would make, carelessly scattered and not covered over. It was almost surely the work of Tyrone.

That and other signs they found along the way convinced MacKenzie those they were after had begun to slow the pace of their journey. And this meant the time needed to catch up to them was steadily growing less. Late in the afternoon he'd even told O'Shaughnessy he now thought it possible their quarry might be less than a day ahead.

The sun was below the western horizon when they came to a series of small streams that meandered between low hillocks, each flowing generally toward the southwest. None of them were deep or swift enough to cause serious delay. But all had to be waded and crossed with care because of the slippery moss-covered rocks that lined their banks and rose up out of the shallow creek beds.

The shadows under the trees were growing deep, and O'Shaughnessy started thinking it might be wiser to stop now and camp for the night, lest darkness make it too hard to find safe footing in such places. But MacKenzie seemed to have no such idea. He meant to waste not a second of what little light remained to further shorten the distance between them and his daughter.

He was making his way across the third or fourth such narrow waterway, with his companion following a few cautious steps behind, when suddenly he let out a yelp of distress. He twisted and flung his arms out in an attempt to keep his balance, but he didn't succeed. With a muttered curse, he fell awkwardly on his side into the slow-moving current.

Still cursing, he rolled over and made an effort to stand up. But his leg seemed to give way, and he plopped back down to a sitting position in the stream.

O'Shaughnessy hurried to kneel beside him. "What is it that's happened, man? Are y' hurt in some way?"

"My ankle!" MacKenzie spoke through gritted teeth. "My foot slipped for an instant from that cursed stone, an' when I tried to recover, I fear I wrenched it!"

O'Shaughnessy reached out to grip his companion under the arms. "Well, let us get you out from the water here an' have a bit o' a look at it."

This turned out to be easier said than done. MacKenzie was the larger and heavier man, and he couldn't put any weight at all on his injured foot. Besides that, there were still the slick, treacherous rocks between them and the bank.

But with the other man's help, he managed to rise to a standing position. Then, with O'Shaughnessy's arm about his waist and by leaning heavily on the smaller man's shoulder, the two of them struggled out of the creek and onto dry land. Only a few feet farther on was a good-sized tree where he could sit on the ground with his back against the rough trunk and his legs out before him.

O'Shaughnessy went to recover his companion's pack and rifle from where he'd been forced to leave them behind in the stream. Then he came and knelt beside MacKenzie's outstretched legs in order to investigate the extent of his injury.

It was almost completely dark by now and not possible to actually "have a look" at the ankle or very much else. But during the Irishman's long years in the Spanish army, he'd had experience with all sorts of hurts and complaints. He quickly removed the soft leather boot from MacKenzie's foot and started to feel knowingly about his lower leg.

MacKenzie grunted softly from time to time as the other man's fingers dug and probed around the various bones. But he offered no comment or complaint. He seemed to realize and accept that O'Shaughnessy knew well enough what he was doing.

At last the Irishman sat back on his heels. "There is nothin' here broken," he said. "That I am able to detect. But 't is surely a nasty sprain for all o' that."

He untucked his shirt and tore strips from its tail; then he moved closer and started do to the same with that of his companion. MacKenzie saw the reason and took over the job himself.

"I will bind this up tight against the swellin' for the present," O'Shaughnessy said. "An' in the span o' another few days you should find yourself able to place weight upon it."

"Another few days!" MacKenzie exploded. "Wi' that Irish villain not a full day before us now! There is no remote chance I will brook such a delay! You must cut me a crutch from some green saplin' close by. An' I will then make my way onward as best as I can!"

O'Shaughnessy didn't respond while he finished wrapping his companion's ankle and replaced his boot. Then he sat back again and shrugged. "It is your ankle," he said mildly. "An' your freedom to suffer. But the cuttin' o' a crutch must needs wait upon daylight. An' in the meanwhile 't will be well to rest yourself now an' preserve all your strength."

He shrugged off his pack and turned to reach inside it. "P'rhaps this will serve to ease the pain a bit an' aid in your slumbers."

MacKenzie felt a cool metal object placed in his hand. It was a small flask. And O'Shaughnessy's next words gave no doubt as to its contents.

"A drop o' the craythur, do y' know. Brought forward from the *Raven* i' the case o' emergencies."

He could sense the Irishman's grin as he twisted off the cap and drank. Then he gave the flask back and did what little he could to make himself comfortable until morning.

36

John Robert and Jeremiah rose at dawn and were already in their saddles before the sun's rays reached their camping place. They made their way north and a bit east now, searching the country for sign but only taking time to dismount when they came to a clearing or some other likely spot where travelers might pause for a nooning or to spend the night.

Late in the morning, at one such place, they found what was left of a fire. It had been carelessly assembled and hastily extinguished, so that the burnt ends of sticks and the white powdering of ashes could easily be seen from horseback.

"Not one of Pa's," John Robert said from where he sat looking down over his horse's neck.

"Not hardly," Jeremiah agreed. "Looks like some tenderfoot's fire. Reckon maybe it was that Tyrone feller, wantin' to dry off a mite after all that rain a couple days ago." He swung down to take a look about the clearing.

"You see any sign he'd got Becky along with him?"

Jeremiah walked a few steps, studying the ground. "Could be. 'Pears like there's maybe two sets of tracks, though kind of hard to tell with all the wiregrass an' pine needles hereabouts."

He pointed to a log near the remains of the fire and the scrape marks on the ground that showed where it was moved. "Feller pulled this over yonder to sit on. Didn't want to get his butt wet, I reckon."

He circled around the ashes and knelt across from the log. "Needles kind of pushed around here, like somebody else might of been sittin' by the fire for a spell." He reached out and carefully bared a patch of earth in front of him.

"Yep! One mighty clear footprint there on the ground! Most surely too small for a man's." He looked up at his brother. "I reckon we just finally managed to come up on the trail of ol' Becky!"

John Robert dismounted and tied the horses at the edge of the clearing. He crossed to where Jeremiah had sat back on his heels and begun to survey the rest of their surroundings. He looked down at the small footprint and then up at the thoughtful frown on his brother's face. After a moment he asked, "What else, you figure?"

"Well, first off, that Tyrone feller seemed to be keepin' his distance, not co-min' too close to where Becky was at."

"Prob'ly a good idea, knowin' our li'l sister."

"I reckon. If I didn't know how Pa felt about Ma, I might of thought he'd had him a fling with a wildcat whenever that gal child got sired." He pointed to the ground. "But I got a notion he'd had her hands tied up too. See those marks yonder? Fingers diggin' into the sand. An' pretty much in back of where I figure she was sittin'."

John Robert glanced down, scowled, and nodded.

They were silent for a few moments. Then Jeremiah pointed at a low shrub a dozen yards away. "Take a closer look at that li'l hawthorn bush over yonder. Seems to be somethin' there in amongst the leaves."

John Robert crossed to the plant and bent to examine it. "Uh-huh. Li'l bit of wool nappin', caught by the thorns." He plucked out the remnant and held it up while continuing his search through the branches. "Couple linen threads 'round about in here too. You reckon he went an' took off his clothes so's to' hang 'em out to dry?"

"Shouldn't wonder." There was a long moment while the brothers met each other's eyes. Then Jeremiah asked, "Anything you see yonder you think might of been Becky's?"

John Robert turned back and made an even more thorough study of the bush. "Nope. Not so far's I can tell." He straightened up. "I don't reckon she'd of ever got shut of her clothes of her own account. It could be he was just willin' to leave bad enough alone."

"'Nother good idea," Jeremiah said grimly. "That feller's bought himself enough trouble already!"

They spent the better part of another hour going over every inch of the clearing. Just outside it, under the trees, they found two more sets of tracks, one coming from the east and the other leading into the forest on the west.

"Pa," John Robert said. "I'd know that long stride of his anywhere."

"Uh-huh. An' in company with that other feller he was travelin' with, I reckon."

"So he's still on their trail. Maybe a day or so behind 'em?"

"Close enough. Give or take a few hours."

"Then I guess it's time we got to followin' 'em." John Robert left the far edge of the clearing and started back to where he'd left their horses. But when he'd covered half the distance, he realized his brother hadn't joined him. He looked over his shoulder and saw Jeremiah on his knees a little deeper into the forest.

"What?" he called. "You find somethin' else?"

"Uh-huh." Jeremiah got slowly to his feet and came toward his brother. "And you ain't goin' to like it."

When they were a few feet apart, he went on in a lower voice: "'Pears like Pa an' us ain't the only ones trailin' folks out here in the wilderness."

John Robert frowned and was silent for a moment. "Injuns?" he asked quietly. Jeremiah nodded without saying a word.

MacKenzie was awake as the first faint traces of daylight began to reveal the black shapes of limbs over his head. He stirred and made an effort to push himself up from where he'd been lying with his back against the tree. But when he shifted the position of his injured leg, he found that the ankle had swollen and grown stiff during the night. He let out a grunt of pain.

"Preserve your strength, lad." O'Shaughnessy had already risen and was squatting a few feet away watching him. "Remain where you are for the nonce, an' just pass me over your knife. I will make shift to go an' prepare that crutch you spoke o' last evenin'. After that we may see how fit you are to rise an' make your way onward."

MacKenzie sighed and did what he was asked. He unsheathed his large knife and handed it hilt first to the Irishman, who offered him a few strips of jerky in return. As he was taking his first bite, O'Shaughnessy rose and disappeared into the woods.

For a time his companion was outside the range of his vision. When he returned, the day was growing brighter, and he was carrying a crutch he'd fashioned out of a slender but sturdy green sapling. He'd stripped off the bark and padded the fork at the top with some Spanish moss and strips of cloth he'd cut from his cloak. It seemed clear this wasn't the first time he'd performed such a task.

MacKenzie put away the water bottle he'd been drinking from and accepted the knife to return it to its sheath. Then, with O'Shaughnessy's arms and shoulders for support, he rose awkwardly to his feet.

His soft leather boot was painfully tight from the swelling and the wrappings. But it did provide a small measure of support, and it would have been impossible to pull on if they'd laid it aside until morning.

He tried a few tentative steps with the crutch and found he was able to manage, though he cursed at the fact that he still couldn't put any weight on his injured ankle. After that, he stood quietly and watched while O'Shaughnessy took up his own equipment and then added MacKenzie's rifle and pack to his burden.

With the rising sun at their backs, they set out once more through the forest, MacKenzie hobbling grimly and the Irishman by his side.

MacKenzie chafed at the enforced slowness of their progress. But his woodsman's senses weren't impaired, and he had little trouble making out the signs left behind by Tyrone and his captive. It seemed these were also proceeding less swiftly than before. There was no longer the sense of urgency he'd noted in his enemy's earlier movements. And he was being even more careless about hiding his trail.

Prudence and wariness had also slowed the MacKenzie brothers' advance. They'd lost little time in deciding to continue their trek on foot, removing their spurs and tying strips of cloth about trace chains and other gear that could cause unwanted noise. The signs had shown that the natives were walking as well.

They had left little obvious evidence of their passing, which was to be expected. But still it had not taken Jeremiah long to become reasonably sure that their numbers were small. Perhaps there were not more than two.

Yet that wasn't any reason to relax their own vigilance. They'd no idea yet whether the natives ahead of them might prove hostile. And two armed Creek warriors, as someone once said, could be quite a few.

Even if their general intentions were friendly, the presence of four fine saddle horses could be a powerful temptation.

37

By comparison with the challenges of the previous days, the final leg of the *Raven*'s voyage to Pensacola felt almost leisurely. She'd succeeded in negotiating the passage between Santa Rosa Island and the mainland without any great difficulty, though progress was slow with frequent soundings and every man watching for shallows and shoals. When darkness arrived, they'd anchored in the waterway and waited for dawn before completing the journey.

It was not much past noon on the following day when they were challenged by a Spanish picket ship near the entrance to the bay. By then they'd hoisted the ensign of the United States, and since the two countries were at peace, the Spanish captain was prepared to accept their presence. Yet he remained wary and was obviously curious about the unusual direction of the schooner's approach.

He and a few of his men were allowed to come on board so they could verify that the Americans carried no contraband and be further assured the visitors were friendly. Kirkland told them briefly about the threat from the British warship and then asked for an audience with the governor of West Florida to more fully explain their arrival.

After the Spaniards had returned to their ship, the *Raven* was escorted into Pensacola Bay proper, under the guns of forts that guarded the harbor. The expanse of water beyond looked even larger than that they'd just come from.

A varied array of vessels could be seen nearby and in the distance, most of them no larger than the *Raven* herself. Some were much smaller: jolly boats and smacks and yawls, even a lateen-rigged dhow of the Arabian type. Many of those clearly were fishing boats or oystermen probing the shallows. But others moved about on unknown tasks, their colorful sails of white, red, and yellow gliding to and fro in the afternoon sun.

It was some three or four miles to the harbor opposite the small village that was the capital of the colony of West Florida. Here they were advised to drop anchor among the bare masts of other vessels rocking gently nearby. They were asked to remain on board until word could be sent as to when—or if—the Spanish governor would see them.

As the sails were being taken in, Kirkland noticed a larger ship at anchor some distance away. She was clearly a merchantman, and from the staff at her taffrail a British ensign fluttered in the breeze. Probably she belonged to the John Forbes Company, an indication that the English firm meant to continue its profitable trade with the Indians despite any prospects of war on the horizon.

It seemed an odd risk to take under the circumstances. But perhaps it was a part of some plan of deception.

The wait for a message from the Spanish governor turned out to be a long one. The afternoon wore on, with no boat approaching the *Raven* and none of those around her seeming to pay her the slightest attention.

Kirkland wasn't happy about the delay. But he knew from experience how slowly the wheels of all government bureaucracies—his own included—were inclined to turn.

He went to his cabin and changed into his dress uniform, just in case the hoped-for summons came sooner than expected. Then he sat down on his bunk and thought through once more what he planned to say to the Spaniards about the British plot to seize their colonies.

He spent no longer than half an hour at this task, for he'd already rehearsed carefully the speech he would make and had no intention of altering it now. His knowledge of Spanish was passable but not fluent, and so he'd enlisted the help of one of his sailors who had been born and raised in the Canary Islands. Any tinkering with what they'd decided on together might only cause unwanted confusion.

Satisfied he'd be able to get through the interview with reasonable assurance, he rose to his feet and went out on deck.

He crossed to the rail and stood there for a time, gazing out over the broad waters of the bay. One way or the other, his mission to West Florida was nearing its end. They'd done what they could about the Indians, though his meeting with two chiefs and one small village might turn out to be useless in the larger picture.

As for the Spanish, he could do no more than warn them of the British threat. He'd be unable to help them in any other way. President Jefferson's insistence on rigid neutrality tied his hands and those of his crew unless they were to come under direct attack. And perhaps even then, since their presence in the Floridas was officially unrecognized by his superiors.

At length he turned away, pausing briefly to glance shoreward with hope but little expectation that he might see a courier boat approaching with a message from the governor. There wasn't, and with nothing else to occupy his time, he shrugged and went below into the salon.

He found Jaynes there ahead of him, seated at the table with what appeared to be an untouched mug of coffee on the stained surface before him. He was now clad in the resplendent dress uniform of a gunnery sergeant of Marines, for it had been decided that he and his commander would serve together as the tiny delegation to the Spanish authorities.

They each nodded a greeting, but no one spoke until Kirkland had gotten coffee for himself and took his seat across the table.

"Not long now," Jaynes said quietly after a few moments.

Kirkland shrugged. "I don't know. These Spaniards seem to have their own ideas about time. We may have to wait several more hours."

"That's likely enough." Jaynes agreed. "But what I meant was for our mission here as a whole. Whatever happens with the Spaniards, we should be free to go on about our own affairs no later than tomorrow." He met Kirkland's eyes. "Any thoughts about what we'll do then?"

Kirkland tasted his coffee and didn't respond immediately. He was almost sure the sergeant knew as well as he did what he personally meant to do.

"There is a matter of unfinished business," he said slowly, "that we left behind us there on the Apalachicola. It's something I can't forget and can't leave be without trying to put it right. I'm going in search of Tyrone and his prisoner. If he's not already in Pensacola, then I'll just set off into the wilderness and hope I can run him to ground there."

Jaynes nodded. Then, after a pause, "And your plan's to do this alone?"

"I couldn't ask anyone else to face charges of desertion. It's a risk I'm willing to take. But the rest of you will have to stay with the ship and make your way to some friendly port. New Orleans or Savannah would be the two I'd recommend."

The sergeant let his eyes roam up to the beams of the low overhead. "I can't say a word for the others," he observed thoughtfully. "But for a fightin' Marine like myself, this voyage has been far too much water and not near enough land." He looked back at Kirkland and grinned. "I think I'll just take a chance on that desertion charge myself. Anyhow, it's not like we're at war and doing it in the face of an enemy."

Kirkland shook his head and smiled. "A sea lawyer's distinction. But I suppose the penalty might be less for an enlisted man who's not expected to know any better." He eyed the sergeant for another moment. "And in any event," he concluded, "if you're fool enough to come with me, I'd be a bigger fool to order you not to!"

The shadows of trees that lined the Bay of Pensacola were stretching long arms across the water when a boat finally arrived with a message from the Spanish governor. It was an invitation for Kirkland and Jaynes to dine with him that evening at his residence. Whatever it was they had to discuss with him could be brought up when the meal was over.

It was hours later and fully dark by the time the two made it back on board the *Raven*. Every man in the schooner's crew was still awake, intently curious to know the outcome of their mission. As their officers climbed up onto the lamplit deck, they were struck by the bemused expressions on both their faces.

At first Kirkland appeared not to notice the men who stood a short distance away in respectful silence. He started aft toward his cabin with his chin lowered as if in deep thought. Sergeant Jaynes's abrupt "Sir?" from behind brought him to a halt.

He turned slowly and looked for a moment into the questioning eyes of his crew, then realized with a sigh that it was no one's job but his own as captain to inform them of the latest startling developments. He came a few steps back toward them.

"Our mission is finally finished," he said. "And I'm proud to say that every man among you has earned a hearty 'Well done!' from myself and from your nation. My written report to Washington will make that abundantly clear." He paused and seemed to have difficulty finding the words to continue.

"As regards the British threat to these Spanish colonies . . . well, that's now over as well. At least for the present." He made a wry face. "There has been a recent and unexpected change in the situation.

"To put it in a nutshell, several months ago the emperor Napoleon of France invaded Portugal and now plans to replace the king of Spain with one of his brothers. The Spanish people won't put up with that, and neither will the British. They intend to send troops to Portugal and support a Spanish rebellion."

Kirkland paused again, then concluded with an ironic shrug. "What that means is . . . Spain and England have now become allies in the war against France!"

There was a stunned silence among the men, and Kirkland took advantage of it to turn away and seek the privacy of his cabin. It would be a minute or two before the realization sank in that two comrades had been killed and a young woman placed in jeopardy over a mission that seemed now to have had no purpose.

There would be more questions then and likely some angry outcries. But Kirkland had no answers for either of those. He'd leave it to Sergeant Jaynes to cope with the emotions of the moment.

In the morning, when everyone had had a chance to calm down and get a good night's rest, he'd gather them all together so decisions could be made about what to do about their future and that of the *Raven*.

In the meantime, he'd his own plans to think about. If, as he more than half expected, these included setting out with Sergeant Jaynes into wild and un-tamed Florida, there would be supplies and equipment to assemble. And if at all possible, a guide to be engaged who was familiar with the country.

Perhaps he might even take a few hours before dawn to snatch some much-needed sleep.

38

John Robert and Jeremiah had spent the night taking turns staying awake to keep watch. In the morning they set out once more on foot. Jeremiah went ahead to search for sign while John Robert brought up the rear with the horses in tow.

Their slower progress was frustrating, since at long last they'd come across their father's trail and it now appeared that he and his companion were no more than a day's ride ahead. But taking the chance of losing the horses, and possibly their scalps, could result in more than frustration.

And from earliest memory, all the MacKenzie offspring had been instilled by their sire with the calm perseverance of the long hunter.

There was little doubt the Indians were following the same trail as themselves. They came upon places where these had paused to study the ground at the white men's' noonings or camps for the night. After the first few times, Jeremiah decided there wasn't a lot of point in delaying their advance for another lengthy scrutiny. As long as he could still make out the trail of the natives, it would be enough to just follow along where it led.

This would save them time in shortening the distance between themselves and their father. But, of course, it would bring them closer to the Indians as well.

And that was a chancy proposition. There was no telling what might happen if the warriors found out they themselves were being followed. The brothers couldn't afford to sacrifice caution for speed. They kept their weapons ready and stepped lightly through the tree-shaded woodland, every sense alert for the slightest noise or movement that might warn them of the presence of others.

John Robert let his brother search the ground ahead for sign. His eyes roamed the forest all around them, with frequent glances back at the ears of their horses. Their senses were generally sharper than humans', and they might well provide the earliest warning of danger.

All in all, it meant for slow going, even without long halts to examine the stopping places of those they trailed. There seemed little chance they would catch up to their father any time in the near future.

Yet, when they paused for a brief rest with the midday sun dappling the ground beneath the trees, Jeremiah whispered that he thought both groups ahead weren't so far off as they'd once supposed. Perhaps as soon as tomorrow . . .

It gave them fresh hope and resolve as they again took up the pursuit. Each began to think more definitely about what the day ahead might bring. With Indians between themselves and their father—who could be unaware of them—and with their sister and her kidnapper somewhere beyond these, there would be no shortage of challenges.

And very likely some fighting.

Which would be just fine with the MacKenzie brothers. They'd had a long and tedious journey during the weeks since they left St. Augustine, each day plagued by doubts and uncertainty. A little clear-cut fighting at the end of it might do well to relieve the tension.

When night finally closed in, they took little trouble about making camp beyond tethering the horses and drawing straws to decide who'd be the first to stretch out on the pine-needle-covered earth for a few restless hours of sleep.

Becky's problem was different from those of everyone behind her. What she wanted desperately was to find some way of further postponing their arrival in Pensacola. She'd thought about it almost constantly during a long and sleepless night.

And finally she'd come up with an idea.

They had left the acorns to soak in the water of the stream overnight, planning to have them for breakfast before setting out again in the morning. When it grew light, Tyrone untied her hands and feet; then he took charge of the rope attached to the noose at her neck so she could walk down to the bank and retrieve them.

She glanced at him surreptitiously while she paused next to the water and tested the ground with a foot. One place seemed soft and crumbly enough for her purpose. She put her full weight on it as she bent to undo the string that was connected to the sack of acorns.

"Oh!'" she cried as the earth gave way and her foot plunged into the water. She sat heavily down on the bank and grabbed her leg, twisting her face into a grimace of pain.

"What is it, lass?" Tyrone took a few steps toward her, then came to a wary halt.

"My ankle! I think I've hurt it!"

For a minute Tyrone seemed torn by indecision. Then he removed his weapons and laid them down some distance away. He came up and knelt beside the girl, who'd now taken her foot from the water and was feeling it tenderly.

"Is it bad, do y' think? Can y' manage to rise?" He offered her his arm.

Becky gripped the arm tightly with both hands, and together they struggled to their feet. "It is not broken, I think. Perhaps I can walk . . ."

She tried a few tentative steps, leaning heavily against him. "Yes. It is painful but I can still put some weight on it. I think it may be all right after a few hours' rest." She looked at him askance. "Perhaps later today . . . or tomorrow . . . "

Tyrone scowled and then nodded. He seemed both angered and relieved that the extent of her injury wasn't worse.

"Well, then," he said with a grudging resignation, "it is rest you shall have."

He took hold of her arm in a firm grip that would discourage any attempt to escape or attack—which she'd no plans to do just at present—and helped her limp up the bank to where their fire had been the previous night. He carefully steered her around the place where he'd left his weapons.

After seating her on the ground, he retied her hands behind her and again fastened the rope with the noose around the bole of a tree. He left her feet unbound while he went to recover the acorns from the stream and then retrieve his pistol and rapier.

Becky sat placidly at the spot where he'd left her and took in a deep breath. Her plan had worked! At least after a fashion. She was still almost helpless: even with her feet free, the idea of trying to shake off the noose and run away into the trees seemed to offer little hope of success. She'd almost surely be recaptured before nightfall.

But she'd gained a few more hours of respite now, perhaps even as much as a day. And with every minute of that, her father would be getting closer. The certainty of this fact fueled and steeled her resolve. Anything else was too terrible to imagine!

The rest of the day was long but for the most part uneventful. She lay down and dozed a little in the morning sun, waking periodically to look about and see what her captor might be doing, most of which seemed to be pacing restlessly.

From time to time he disappeared into the wooded grove that lined the edge of the clearing. At other times he descended to the bank of the stream and gazed off across it for long minutes at a stretch.

What his thoughts might be during these seemingly aimless wanderings she couldn't guess and preferred not to imagine.

In the afternoon Tyrone came to sit on the grass nearby and asked about the state of her ankle. She told him she was feeling less pain than before but still didn't think she could walk for any great distance. She demonstrated by letting him pull her to her feet and then essaying a few halting steps with a pitiful groans and grimaces.

Tyrone sighed and nodded, agreeing it would be better to spend another night in this spot and continue on in the morning.

After they resumed their seats, there followed long periods of silence interspersed by occasional interludes of quiet conversation. Again her captor talked mostly of himself and his glowing plans for their future. For her part, Becky spoke little, and when she did, it was with a shy coyness that she hoped would encourage the man to believe she was actually growing to like him.

During the anxious hours of darkness, she slept fitfully and infrequently but was surprised and thankful to find that her self-proclaimed fiancé was keeping his promise. Whether it was because of her feigned injury or some twisted notion of honor, at nightfall he simply made himself comfortable on the grass a respectful distance away and, as near as she could tell, didn't stir from the spot until dawn came to brighten the leaves overhead.

39

When it finally grew light, there was brisk chill in the air, and a ribbon of fog marked the path of the winding stream below the hillock where Tyrone and Becky had spent their second night.

Though the weather had been sunny and mild during the greater part of each recent day, the mornings tended to be cold and damp. Tyrone woke at dawn, sat up with a muttered curse, and then quickly rose to his feet. He wasted little time grabbing up his weapons and throwing his cloak around his shoulders before hurrying to the ashes of their nightly fire. He knelt there, stirring and blowing on the coals to kindle them back to life.

Becky was wide awake and watching him.

When he'd added some sticks to the fire and seen the flames flicker around them and then spread out into a cheerful blaze, he added more fuel and sat back on his heels. A minute or two later, he turned his attention to his captive.

He grinned when he noticed her attentive eyes upon him. "A good day to you, lass! An' how does the wounded limb o' my fair companion feel on this brisk an' promisin' mornin'?"

"Much better, thank you." Becky had decided that trying to feign complete disability for another day might be pushing her luck too far. She could still use the excuse to slow their pace, however. "There's only a slight tenderness and stiffness now. And I think some of that may be worked out after I've moved around for a bit."

"Excellent! So do y' believe you might essay to find us a bit o' provender for our mornin's repast? I will confess that yesterday's scant handfuls o' acorns did not provide much lastin' sustenance."

"I believe I may. There are still plenty of cattail roots and greens close by. And if I move slowly and carefully . . ."

He got to his feet and came to untie her hands. "Well enough. We'll share a bite o' breakfast, an' then it's off to the west again wi' no further delays. Just a few short days longer wi' clear skies an' fair weather should see us aboard ship an' free o' this dolorous colony forever!"

Becky sat quietly rubbing her wrists while Tyrone went to release the longer rope that tethered her noose to the tree. He turned back with the rope in his hands.

"Arise now an' stir yourself, my lass. Once you've fetched our mornin's provisions, we'll bring 'em back by the fire an' spend only a brief while consumin' 'em. No lost minutes burnin' off cactus spines this day. By the time the sun has approached the tops o' the trees, I mean to be well upon our way!"

Becky let out a faint groan as she pushed herself up from the ground. Then she made her way slowly down to the stream while making sure that Tyrone, who followed several yards behind, could see her noticeable limp when she placed one foot before the other.

She knelt to pluck cattails from a bend in the creek and then rose painfully to move farther along to where a green cluster of watercress could be seen hugging the bank. Behind her there suddenly came an angry shout from the forest that bordered their camping place. She knew that voice!

"Tyrone, y' black-hearted villain! Free that girl on the instant an' turn to face y'r reckonin'!"

Becky spun on her heel to see her father and another man standing at the edge of the clearing with the dark shadows of the trees beyond them. The shouted threat she'd just heard seemed disappointingly empty in that moment. Her father was leaning heavily on a crutch, and his long rifle was slung uselessly over the shoulder of his companion—who she now realized was the Irishman Michael O'Shaughnessy.

Tyrone turned swiftly toward the new arrivals and reached to seize the pistol from his sash. As he drew it out and raised it to point at MacKenzie, Becky gave out a loud cry in the wild hope of distracting him. At the same time, her hands were clawing desperately at the noose around her neck.

It was less the sound of her voice than the sharp tugs on the rope in his free hand that drew Tyrone's attention. He glanced quickly in her direction and caught a brief glimpse of a suddenly unhurt and agile young woman as she threw the noose aside and plunged into the fog-shrouded creek to make a dash for the opposite shore.

He hesitated no more than a few seconds to reach a decision. The fleeing girl would keep until he had time to run her to ground. The immediate threat was before him. He turned his attention and his pistol back on those foes and instantly pulled the trigger.

MacKenzie had used the brief delay to take partial cover behind a nearby tree. O'Shaughnessy remained in the open, holding his back erect and facing his enemy like the well-trained soldier he was. He'd only shed the encumbrances of rifle, packs, and cloak before drawing his rapier free of its scabbard. The polished steel caught glittering highlights in the rays of the rising sun.

Hitting either man at a distance with one shot from a flintlock pistol was a doubtful thing at best. But as it occurred, there was no risk of it at all. The abortive snap of the weapon's lock sounded loud in the morning stillness. In his earlier haste, Tyrone had failed to replace the previous day's charge with fresh, dry powder. And the night's heavy dew had done its work.

He threw the worthless weapon aside while voicing a bitter curse. Then he flung off his cloak and reached to draw his own blade from its sheath.

O'Shaughnessy was already coming toward him with slow and measured steps.

Tyrone raised his rapier in an ironic salute accompanied by a sneering smile. "Methinks you overrate yourself, me boyo. There was a time I was reputed the finest swordsman in all o' the Caribbean. Six strong men's lives were cut short in as many months by a thrust from this cold bit o' steel."

"Indeed?" O'Shaughnessy slowed but didn't halt his advance. "But surely all that was some little while before I arrived in these Floridas!"

In another few moments, and without further words, they'd come near enough for both combatants to assume the en garde position. The two blades crossed.

40

The grassy clearing rang with the metallic sounds of deadly combat. The tip of each blade seemed to move of its own accord—circle, beat, remise, reprise, attack, and riposte—all too quickly for an untrained eye to follow.

At first Tyrone sought a rapid finish to the duel. His point reached out, threatening one way, a quick beat, and a sudden change of line to attack from another direction. His style was confident and aggressive, striking his enemy's blade sharply and often in hopes of weakening his wrist and opening the way for a fatal thrust.

To his surprise and consternation, O'Shaughnessy seemed unaffected by the force of the assault. He parried each thrust and feint with what appeared almost casual ease. The tip of his rapier flicked left and right, above and below, seldom for more than an inch or so but always deftly turning every try by his opponent to bring his own point to bear.

After several minutes, Tyrone disengaged and stepped back, breathing hard and angered by the fact that his foe looked scarcely winded.

"I see that you have a bit o' skill wi' the blade after all," he said grudgingly. "But all the better for that. 'T will make it a more worthy test o' my own ability. An' give me the more pleasure when my steel finds your heart!"

For the first time, O'Shaughnessy smiled faintly. But he said nothing, merely waiting with his guard up for Tyrone to resume the attack.

Which he did almost immediately, though with more caution than before. His point probed, beat lightly, and circled, seeking now to draw his opponent into committing to an attack of his own: some incautious thrust that would lend itself to a swift and deadly riposte. The sounds of the battle grew less strident, only whispering rasps of metal on metal punctuated by occasional bell-like taps.

At times Tyrone would retreat a few steps and slip to one side, offering O'Shaughnessy a further invitation to respond with rash overconfidence.

But none of it was to any avail. The other man's skill with a blade seemed matched only by his unruffled patience.

MacKenzie had come out from behind the tree to watch with admiring fascination this deadly chess match. He could hardly follow the swift interplay of sharp steel points as they threatened and responded and returned to the attack. It seemed to last for an endless time, though likely it was not more than a quarter of an hour. Neither swordsman looked able to gain any advantage, and the contest could be destined to end in exhaustion for one of them or both.

But then he began to realize that O'Shaughnessy was drawing blood. His blade moved so swiftly that the only signs of this result were red blotches and streaks that appeared without warning on Tyrone's white shirt and bare flesh: a nick in the ear that dripped blood on his shoulder, a faint stripe lower down, a spreading stain on the sleeve of his sword arm. And a dark spot over the knee on one leg of his breeches, which seemed to be growing larger.

None of these wounds was deep; they were barely more than scratches to any casual observer. But each one oozed blood, and MacKenzie knew that in time such loss could weaken even the strongest man. And those pricks in the thigh and forearm must surely slow the reactions of any skillful swordsman.

Tyrone knew it too. His time to seize a victory was rapidly growing shorter. When O'Shaughnessy's point reached the side of his face and drew a livid line from cheekbone to chin, he uttered a roar of rage and went at his tormentor with renewed force and violence. He clearly meant to end the fight now, before the combined effect of his hurts might fatally sap his strength.

O'Shaughnessy had to give ground under the heavy onslaught of repeated blows. Yet he retreated calmly and with measured steps. Not once did his rapier point falter in its deft movements to parry and turn aside each of his enemy's attacks.

And then he fell.

He hadn't dared to take his eyes for an instant from Tyrone and his slashing blade. When he came to the place where the nightly fires had been, one foot chanced to come down on the end of an unburnt log. It rolled beneath him, and his legs went out from under his body. He hit the ground heavily on his back.

Tyrone voiced a triumphant cry and leaped forward to take advantage. But with bare seconds to spare, O'Shaughnessy rolled over twice and came up on one knee. He caught the other's downward thrust with the guard of his blade and forced it aside. Then, without breaking contact, he drove his foe relentlessly back while rising to his feet.

MacKenzie had caught his breath and watched helplessly while this brief drama unfolded, unable with his crutch to move rapidly or offer any assistance.

And then he thought of his rifle, temporarily forgotten with all his attention on the deadly contest before him. His eyes searched the ground, and he spotted it a dozen yards away, partly hidden behind a stand of palmettos. He started to limp clumsily in that direction.

The abandoned weapon might not be of any use to him. Even if he could keep his balance while lowering himself to take it up, he'd almost surely need to replace the priming with fresh powder before it could be fired. And then he'd have to wonder if the main charge hadn't succumbed to the morning dampness like that in Tyrone's pistol.

But if worst came to worst, it could be his only defense against a victorious and vengeful enemy.

In the meantime, the desperate swordplay continued in the middle of the grassy clearing. The mist was now gone from the creek bed, and the rising sun showed full on the sweat-stained faces of the two antagonists.

O'Shaughnessy was retreating in a broad circle, yielding only grudgingly to Tyrone's resumed assault. At times his own point flicked out with a sudden riposte that often found its mark. His adversary's white shirt now showed red in a dozen places, and a shallow cut on his forehead leaked blood that threatened to blind him.

Both men were starting to show signs of tiring. Tyrone was breathing in ragged gasps, and O'Shaughnessy's nimble footwork seemed a step slower than it had been formerly.

Yet neither displayed the slightest willingness to pause or disengage for even an instant. The flashing steel moved to and fro and rang with grim persistence while both duelists strove without success to create that one vital opening.

Then, with startling suddenness, Tyrone took several steps back and lowered the point of his blade. He clutched at his breast with his free hand and let out an agonized moan. His mouth opened and closed as if he were struggling to catch his breath. A few moments later, his eyes rolled up and he slowly sank to the ground.

O'Shaughnessy watched with stunned surprise, and his sword arm started to drop. A heart attack? It wasn't beyond reason, given the man's age and their strenuous expenditure of effort. He took a step forward.

MacKenzie, now kneeling to take up his rifle, called out an urgent warning. He knew his old enemy far better than did his recent companion.

And sure enough, the moment O'Shaughnessy came within reach, his "stricken" foe managed a sudden and complete recovery. He sat up, and his blade shot forward from where he'd held it across his body.

It was only unthinking reflex that enabled his would-be victim to parry the thrust. Nor did the instant riposte that followed require any conscious thought. Tyrone's eyes opened wide with surprise as the blade sank deep into his exposed chest. When it was withdrawn, he sank back again, this time in unfeigned agony.

A pink froth appeared on his lips as he stared balefully up at his adversary. "Done for!" he muttered with a more than a hint of disbelief. "Done for in the end by a mongrel sot of a shanty Irishman!" He might have added some curses, but his words were cut short by a convulsive cough that was followed by a spate of blood.

MacKenzie was struggling to his feet with the crutch in one hand and his rifle gripped in the other. But he already knew there was no need for haste.

Even from this distance he could readily see that his longtime foe had breathed his last.

41

O'Shaughnessy gazed down at the body of the man he had killed and took a deep breath. Then he turned away and crossed the clearing on somewhat shaky legs. It had been a long time since he'd had to maintain the fencing stance for so many minutes. When he came to a tree festooned with Spanish moss, he pulled a clump of it down and started to clean his sword.

MacKenzie watched him for a minute, then put the fork of the crutch under his arm and began to limp in that direction. He almost lost his precarious balance and tumbled to the ground when he was struck by a hurtling body that ran headlong out from among the trees. It threw its arms around his neck and pressed so tightly against him that it was several seconds before he could catch his breath.

"Father!"

He let his rifle fall to the ground so he could wrap his free arm about her waist. "Rebecca!" he managed to gasp.

Neither spoke again for several long minutes. Becky simply clung to him with her face pressed hard against his chest. At last he disengaged and looked down into her face. Her eyes were filled with tears.

"Are y' all right, girl? Are y' hurt at all?" He hesitated. "Did that damnable beast . . . ?" He couldn't bring himself to finish the question.

"No." She shuddered and shook her head. "No, he did not. Thanks to a merciful Providence and more luck than perhaps I deserve." She saw no need to tell him about Tyrone's scheme to marry her and spirit her off to Ireland. The man was dead and his plans along with him. The rest was something she would remember—if at all—as only a very bad dream.

"As for me," she went on with a faint shrug, "I guess I'm about as well and fit as might be expected. Under the circumstances."

MacKenzie gripped her shoulder and held her at arm's length, looking her up and down from head to toe. Her hair was in disarray, and her face was streaked with tears and dirt. The men's trousers she wore were soaked and dripping from splashing both ways across the stream. But he saw no signs of lasting damage. He did notice her chafed wrists and the band of raw, red skin that encircled her neck. He could guess at the reasons but might ask more about them later.

O'Shaughnessy had sheathed his rapier and come up to stand a few feet away. When Becky turned toward him, he made a courtly bow. "It is a very great pleasure to find you safe an' hale, young miss. There has been more than a bit o' worry among your shipmates this long week past." He smiled. "Not only the two o' us here but those that duty has called to be elsewhere."

Becky responded to the bow with equal formality, returning the smile and holding out her hand. O'Shaughnessy took it and pressed it to his lips.

"I'm very grateful for your concern," she said with a faint catch in her voice. "Every one of you."

Then her knees seemed to grow weak, and she gripped her father's arm with both hands. He brought her close and held her while she looked up into his eyes.

"I knew you would come," she said quietly. "I never doubted it for a second. It was almost the only thing that helped me stay the course. I didn't know when, or if you'd be alone or with . . . others." She paused and looked at O'Shaughnessy. "But if you were to have only one companion, I'm awfully glad you chose the one that you did!"

MacKenzie glanced down at the crutch and his injured ankle. "'T wasn't entirely a matter o' my choosin'," he confessed. "But today I am even better pleased than yourself the choice was made!"

O'Shaughnessy gave a modest shrug and opened his mouth to respond. But before he could, there were sounds from the wooded grove some several yards away. All eyes turned in that direction.

Two Creek Indians emerged from the leafy shadows and stood in the open with arms across their chests. MacKenzie recognized them instantly, as did O'Shaughnessy a moment or two later. The Irishman put his hand on the hilt of his rapier.

These were the chiefs from the Indian village they'd visited earlier. Their names, as MacKenzie recalled, were Nah-ta-lah and Wa-tah-hoya. They were looking thoughtfully around at the scene before them and seemed in no hurry to break the silence.

MacKenzie pushed Becky gently aside and took a few halting steps toward them on his crutch. Before he could ask in their language what they wanted, other sounds could be heard from someplace behind them.

"It's all right, Pa!" came a voice from the shadows. "Turns out they're right peaceful Injuns. Been that way ever since we been followin' 'em!"

Both Becky and MacKenzie knew the voice well.

And MacKenzie wasn't as surprised as some might have guessed to see John Robert and Jeremiah stride out from the forest to clasp his hand. They were, after all, his own sons. And the MacKenzie blood had its way of breeding true.

Their sister greeted both of them with smiling hugs. Her tears had ended some minutes ago, but it was all she could do now to keep them from flowing again.

MacKenzie looked over at the two Creek chiefs, who hadn't stirred from their places since they'd first appeared. Nor had they spoken. They'd merely stood watching in silence the happy family gathering.

He separated himself from the others and limped across to stand before them a few feet away. They lifted their hands in a sign of peace, and MacKenzie did the same.

"You have traveled a long path," Wa-tah-hoya said, "since last we met. The young woman is your daughter?" MacKenzie nodded. "She must be very precious to you to risk such a hazardous journey on her behalf."

"She is," MacKenzie replied simply.

"And the other? The one who traveled with you? He is a relation as well?"

"No. He is a friend. But a very fine friend, I am proud to say."

"A brave man. And a mighty warrior, skilled beyond our ken with the long knife. His medicine is strong."

"Yes," MacKenzie agreed. "Far stronger that I once had believed."

"It is good. I think your medicine is strong as well. You are a skillful and determined tracker of men. You have held to your purpose for long days without pause. Even after the storm and in spite of your mishap."

Wa-tah-hoya fell silent and let his eyes go to the others in the clearing, studying them thoughtfully for several long minutes. "There are more among your people of the same sort as you?" he asked.

"Many more. This is a land that oft brings out all the best that is in a man." MacKenzie paused and glanced over his shoulder at the sprawled body of Tyrone. "An' sometimes the worst, I will confess."

Wa-tah-hoya nodded gravely. He said nothing more but simply raised his hand again as if in benediction and turned away. In moments he and his companion had disappeared among the shadows of the forest, and MacKenzie stood alone.

Nah-ta-lah had not spoken a word during the brief interview. His face had remained impassive, but MacKenzie had the impression that his own responses to the older man's questions had given him much food for thought. Perhaps this was true for both of them.

42

"What did those two have to say for themselves?" Jeremiah asked when his father had returned to join him and the others.

"Not so very much. Wa-tah-hoya asked some questions about ourselves an' our kind. An' he spoke o' our medicine." MacKenzie looked over at O'Shaughnessy and smiled. "He said you were a mighty warrior."

"That he is," John Robert agreed. "We watched the best part of that fight from back yonder in the trees—us an' the Injuns."

"You all came here together?"

"Met up with 'em a hour or so back. They'd figured out we were behind 'em an' just waited a spell 'til we got close enough to talk. Lucky for us they weren't feelin' warlike. Just had 'em a curiosity about what you-all were up to an' how it all would turn out."

"An' wished to learn how strong was our medicine, I've no great doubt. I believe they went away from here satisfied on that score."

Jeremiah's brow furrowed. "You reckon that means there won't be any Injun war startin'?"

"No' in the near future, I'm guessin', though the future is never a certain prospect." MacKenzie shrugged. "There will always remain danger o' it in the months an' years ahead."

"Well, then let's just be grateful for what we have today." Becky took her father's arm in one hand and John Robert's in the other. "We're all of us safe and together here at last. And this would be a fine place to camp and rest up for several days. If only"—she looked across at the body of her former abductor, and a lingering note of bitterness crept into her otherwise cheerful manner—"someone would dispose of the garbage!"

John Robert and Jeremiah went off to lead the horses into the clearing and then set about digging a grave some little distance away in order to carry out the task their sister had requested. When they were finished, the fire had been replenished and everyone shared a limited meal consisting of what foods could still be found locally, together with all that was left of the supplies the four men had brought.

It was clear that if they were to remain in this place any longer, some hunting would need to be done. And the MacKenzie brothers were more than ready to oblige. They set out on foot that same afternoon to see what they could find.

Their father remained seated comfortably on the grass with his daughter and O'Shaughnessy beside him. None of them spoke very much at first, just letting the bright afternoon sun warm their tired bodies and help put the trials of past days behind them.

Finally MacKenzie looked at the man sitting next to him. "Y' know, I chanced to hear the words Tyrone said to y' there at the last. He named y' a mongrel. Yet y' told me once y've the blood o' Irish kings in y'r veins. I wonder if that might ha' made a difference to his overweenin' pride durin' the battle."

O'Shaughnessy shrugged. "No more difference than it does to me, I'll wager. 'T would o' been more to the point had he known that in younger days I served as fencin' master at the military institute in Toledo." He smiled faintly. "Though I believe he may o' garnered some hint o' that in the minutes before he died."

The Irishman fell silent for a minute or two and then went on reflectively, "It is a different world out here in these western lands. Mongrel the man called me, and i' truth it is a mongrel I am. Like many another on this side o' the world. For didn't my father win my own dear mother at dice in a Guadalupe tavern?!"

Becky had been listening to the conversation with interest that now became outrage. "Your mother was the stake in a game of chance? Like some common chattel or slave, with no say in the matter at all?!"

"The practice was common enough in that place an' time," O'Shaughnessy said. He gave her a wry smile. "Daughters, y' see, were never thought o' great worth to families wi' much hard work to be done. But then afterward, it did not take my sire long to reveal his true feelin's an' gain the love o' my mother. The years they spent together were as happy as any wedded life might be. 'T was a long an' profitable union." He spread his hands apart and bowed from the waist. "As you may witness from the outcome!"

Becky just scowled at him and shook her head. Then she folded her arms and looked away.

They rested in that place for several days, recovering their strength and taking advantage of the MacKenzie brothers' hunting ability. Free at last of Tyrone and his "leash," Becky enjoyed exploring the nearby forest and the banks of the creek, often bringing back native foods upon her return.

MacKenzie took part in none of this activity. He simply relaxed by a small fire in the clearing, sometimes alone but more often in company with his friend and members of his family. His ankle quickly improved with this welcome inactivity, and before long he was able to hobble about the area without his crutch, happily supervising and offering unsought advice about the activities of his offspring. They endured it with smiling patience, content to bask in the reassuring glow of his well-meant meddling.

On the third day they received a surprise. Lieutenant Kirkland and Sergeant Jaynes arrived from the southwest, along with a buckskinned trapper they'd engaged as a guide. Everyone was pleased at this latest reunion. But MacKenzie couldn't help noticing that the smiles of his daughter had seemed the broadest.

At dinner that night it was decided that after another day's rest for themselves and the newcomers, they would all set out together on the way to Pensacola. As it turned out, Kirkland's crew had chosen not to abandon their captain, voting instead to remain in harbor aboard the *Raven* until he and Jaynes could manage to return. It meant the MacKenzies could look forward to a leisurely return voyage to St. Augustine in relative comfort.

There were only four horses here for the eight of them. But this meant no hardship to O'Shaughnessy and the trapper, who spurned the unaccustomed punishment to their backsides in favor of finishing the journey on foot. Everyone but MacKenzie and Becky agreed that father and daughter should be mounted, while the others took turns either riding or walking.

Once the evening meal was over, MacKenzie sat with O'Shaughnessy in the flickering glow from a somewhat larger fire than he himself would have built, smoking pipes thoughtfully provided by the latest arrivals. The rest were scattered about here and there, talking quietly or just savoring the peaceful stillness of the night.

Kirkland and Becky sat beside one another, barely within the circle of light from the fire. MacKenzie's attention was drawn to them frequently as they gazed into each other's eyes and spoke in whispers about topics unknown. O'Shaughnessy watched his companion. There was a faint smile of amusement on his lips as he took in the situation with tolerant understanding.

After a time, the two young people both got to their feet, shared a lingering glance, and joined hands. Then they turned away from the fire and strolled slowly back among the dark trees.

MacKenzie uttered a sharp grunt and started to rise.

O'Shaughnessy put a gentle hand on his arm. "Leave them be," he said quietly. "There are others here who'll have an eye out for danger. An' surely the swain an' his lady deserve some small minutes to themselves."

When MacKenzie scowled at him, he grinned. "An' you yourself know if yon Kirkland were any less of a man than yourself, your fair daughter would never o' favored him wi' a second glance!"

MacKenzie grudgingly settled back where he was. "Aye," he grumbled, "that is all very well. But if it should chance he's of a mind to prove himself more than that man this night"—he smote the ground with his fist—"I swear by the Almighty I will kill him with my own two hands!"

HISTORICAL NOTES

BRITISH DESIGNS ON FLORIDA

As Becky MacKenzie explains, the British had long sought to incorporate the whole of North America (east of the Mississippi, at any rate) into their worldwide empire. Major incursions were made into Spanish Florida by the English governors of South Carolina (1702–1703) and Georgia (1740) with little success. But in 1763, following the end of the Seven Years' War, it appeared they had finally achieved their goal. Spain ceded East Florida and West Florida (see below) to Britain to become its fourteenth and fifteenth American colonies. The British had already seized Canada from the French some six years earlier.

Unfortunately for the Brits, they lost those colonies only twenty years later (together with the other thirteen) as a result of the American Revolution. But they never lost hope of getting all fifteen of them back.

While the plot described in this novel is fiction, it is completely plausible in the view of the author. Spain and England were at war from 1796 until 1802, and a seaborne invasion of the Floridas once seemed imminent. During this time there actually was a minor invasion by Creek Indians under the direction of William Augustus Bowles, a British adventurer. He was betrayed, captured, and imprisoned. But the two nations were at war again as early as 1804. This came to an end after the Spanish fleet was destroyed (along with that of the French) during the Battle of Trafalgar.

Napoleon's ill-advised placement of his brother Joseph on the throne of Spain and his subsequent invasion of the peninsula in 1808 to punish the rebellious citizens changed everything dramatically. The British decided to enter the fray to support the "rightful monarch" (thereby gaining a foothold on the Continent), and the two former enemies immediately became allies.

Yet the British never completely abandoned their hopes for a North American empire. Many of them viewed the War of 1812 as a long-awaited opportunity, and their troops did seize Pensacola briefly in the course of that war.

THE CASTILLO DE SAN MARCOS

Begun in 1671 to replace an earlier wooden fort (the eighth of these in St. Augustine's history!), the Castillo de San Marcos was constructed entirely of coquina rock quarried on nearby Anastasia Island. This substance consists of tiny shells bound together with limestone and is porous enough to absorb cannon balls without cracking from their force. The *Castillo* was never captured by an enemy in battle, although it was besieged on several occasions by the British and others.

Much as described in the story at the time represented (1808), the fort had suffered considerable neglect over the years. But efforts had been made by the recent Spanish governors to repair as much of the structure as possible given their limited funds and available manpower.

EAST AND WEST FLORIDA

The territory was divided into two colonies by the Spanish, separated by the Apalachicola River. West Florida extended all the way to the Mississippi and included the settlement at Mobile as well as Pensacola. When the British took possession in 1763, they kept this arrangement, with two separate governors and two colonial councils.

THE JOHN FORBES COMPANY

Formerly the Panton-Leslie Company and renamed after William Panton died at sea in 1801, this organization maintained a virtual trade monopoly with the Indians in Florida from the mid-1700s until 1816. Its trading posts could be found as far south as Spalding's Upper Store (present-day Volusia on the upper St. Johns), as far north as the Georgia border, and as far west as Pensacola, where it ultimately established its headquarters.

"PICK AN' WISK"

The pick and whisk was a small wire implement usually looped around one of the buttons of an infantryman's uniform. It had a point at one end and a brush at the other and was used to clean the touch hole and priming pan of a flintlock musket.

THE "SECOND SPANISH PERIOD" (1783–1821)

When the Floridas were restored to the Spanish Crown (see above), that nation was in a much weaker condition than it had been in earlier centuries. Impoverished by runaway inflation from years of bringing home massive amounts of South American silver and gold, Spain now found itself without adequate resources to support its vast colonial empire. Throughout the New World it was proving difficult, if not impossible, to maintain any kind of reasonable civil or military control. In the Floridas there were constant incursions by pirates, outlaws, foreign adventurers (including Americans), and peaceful immigrants from the new United States who sought fresh lands to farm and settle.

THE SPANISH HIBERNIA REGIMENT

The Regimento Hibernia was first organized in 1709 and consisted almost entirely of Irish "wild geese" who had left their homeland to escape British oppression. It continued in Spanish service until 1818, when it was disbanded at the request of the British—who by then were the allies of Spain.

The regiment took part in the invasion of West Florida during the American Revolution (at a time when Spain, as well as France, had allied themselves with the Americans). Its attack and capture of British Pensacola was among its more notable accomplishments. Its commander at the time was Colonel Enrique White, who was subsequently appointed governor of West Florida and later of East Florida.

SEMINOLE INDIANS

The "Spanish Indians" (mostly Apalachees and Timucuans) who formerly occupied North Florida had been drastically reduced in numbers by disease and the rampaging British invasions of the early 1700s. By the middle of that century, few of them were left.

Into this "population vacuum" came wandering bands of Lower Creeks, who gathered up some of the free-ranging Spanish cattle and established settlements of their own. Most came seeking freedom and independence from the large and rigidly authoritarian Creek Nation to the north. (One suggested translation of the word "Seminole" is "those who live apart.") In time this separation became more firmly established, and the Seminoles were augmented by members of other tribes (most notably the Yamassees from South Carolina).

Yet, for a long time, most white men failed to recognize the distinction between these groups. One of the lesser-known sources of the Seminoles' resistance to their relocation to Oklahoma during the 1830s was that they were to be settled on the same reservation as the Creeks, who greatly outnumbered them and had by then become their deadly enemies!

(Incidentally, the term "Black Seminole" is for the most part a misnomer— again owing to the white man's ignorance. Many escaped slaves settled in Florida near the Seminoles and lived alongside them in peaceful coexistence. But almost none of them were ever inducted into the tribe. The Negroes fought as *allies* during the Second Seminole War, having perhaps more reason than the Indians to drive the slaveholding interlopers out.)

SUSCEPTIBILITY OF (SOME) SPANISH SOLDIERS TO BRIBES

Spanish Florida was a military backwater for most of its history. During the Second Spanish Period (see above), it became even worse. The *situado* (government subsidy) was usually late and always insufficient. Soldiers might go for months without pay, and sometimes they went without food as well.

Under these circumstances, it's no surprise that many of those stationed in Florida, who tended to be in the lower stratum of the Spanish army to start with, tended to look after their own interests before those of their mother country. Governor after governor complained that their troops were ill trained, dishonest, and insubordinate. Yet they always seemed to prove themselves steady enough in battle. So who could blame them if they took advantage of a little "supplemental income" whenever it became available?

ABOUT THE AUTHOR

Lee Gramling is a sixth-generation Floridian who was inspired by the tales of the Florida frontier he heard from his grandparents and by the westerns of Louis L'Amour. After a lengthy hiatus from writing, he is now spending his retirement years trying to make up for lost time. He lives in Gainesville, Florida.